David Muller

Of Scottish ancestry, David Muller was born and raised in Germiston, South Africa, and educated at the Sacred Heart College in Johannesburg. Although an engineer by profession, he started writing during the Second World War, while serving in the Royal Navy. Since then, he has written mainly for magazines and the radio.

Whitey

David Muller

RWS

Ravan Writers Series

Published by Ravan Press
PO Box 145 Randburg 2125
South Africa

First published in 1977
Second edition 1995

ISBN 0 86975 468 8

Cover design: Insight Graphics Pretoria
Cover photograph: Used with the kind permission of *The Star* Johannesburg

Printed by Galvin & Sales Cape Town
(0129)

For Pagan

This is a work of fiction. All the characters are imaginary and bear no resemblance to, nor have any connection with any persons who might be either living or dead.

Although the locale and background are authentic, La Residence Stilhuis and the Nest of the Giant Rodent are composite reconstructions of places that existed in District Six before the area was re-zoned and partially demolished.

D.M.

PART ONE

Out of the Black Cotton Night

1

i

He returned from the stygian absence of amnesia, to find himself in this place; a grassy, treey, flowery place that was not at all like the usual gloomy places where the horries get at you when the booze has destroyed all the vitamins in your system, and you are withdrawing and crying out for the drink you cannot get, and the things come. This place was not like that at all. It was splashed by bright sunlight, and there was colour and movement beneath the sky-high trees, with lots of big birds scratching round for food and doing mating-dances. Beneath the trees, and in them, were a number of rodents: big six-feet-high animals with quick bushy tails. The rodents on the ground were standing on their hind legs, accepting food from the giant two-legged creatures that were milling about the place, cracking earth-coloured pods and making awful shrieking noises.

It was an interesting scene, he felt, if peculiar, for he was so small: hardly the size of the kewpie-doll that was sitting beside him. He smiled at the kewpie, for over the years he had become quite accustomed to its presence, though he had been terrified by its first sudden appearance on the bedside locker in the 'drying-out' ward of the State Hospital. But the doll had never caused him any harm or grief, and he had come to the conclusion that the thing could only be the manifestation of his romantically harmless alter ego which somehow became detached at times like this, when he was on one hell of a bender.

The kewpie was a curious creature, given to logic and reason. Acting on the suggestions of its squeaky voice, he had gotten out of many a tight corner whilst drifting through the fantastic, often violent sub-world of alcoholism.

For a while, idly wondering where he was and where he had come from, he lay watching the activities of the various creatures. But then, it seemed to him, a couple of the younger giants had spotted him in the cave of bushes where he lay, were, in fact, bending closer and peering at him with cold curious eyes and pointing jeering fingers in his face, and he became terrified that one of them might step closer and tramp on his small head; or worse, one of the rodents might decide to gobble him up. The fear mounted to a point of horror and he opened his mouth to scream, then, blessedly, the hemisphere of the soap-bubble began to descend, and he melted away into darkness, and in his mind the voice of the kewpie urged him to put off his wheels and float for a couple of harries of jupe*. And he knew that this was the thing to do: this was what he needed to escape from the creatures beyond the dark curtain of his mind.

Safely locked in his mind, conscious of neither time nor space, in a state of total suspension, his soul flickered fitfully in its sphere of multi-coloured light, ever shifting, like a soap-bubble floating in midday space.

And then, in what seemed no time at all, he found himself in another park-like place, and with him was this Coloured fellow who said that his name was Boon. They were sitting with their back to a fence and standing between them were two wine bottles, the one almost empty, which explained his return from the soap-bubble world of his mind. He knew that he had returned — for the time being, anyway — because everything was perfectly normal. The giant beings, the birds and the rodents had vanished, and the kewpie was not to be seen. Some twenty metres away, across the paved pathway, on the green grass, a bunch of jolly kids and their guardians were feeding nuts to a family of nervous squirrels, and there were a few pigeons pecking about the place and doing mating-dances. There was something vaguely familiar about the scene, but his mind was unable to grasp and clarify it. It was like the stories these reincarnation blokes tell you about arriving in a totally strange place, and having the eerie conviction that you had been there before. He did not dwell on the matter: it was of little importance, since he was comfortably seated on the grass beneath some old oak-trees, in the company of Boon and a couple of bottles.

Boon, his new-found companion, was wearing a jacket and a pair of shoes which were also vaguely familiar. After a closer study of the gear, he decided that some time ago it had belonged to himself. This notion was substantiated by the fact that he was unshod and in his shirt sleeves — a condition of undress that is equally unimportant when you are sitting in a pleasant park on a balmy evening, drinking wine. He tossed the puzzle of the clothing aside and grinned happily at Boon, who had a smashed nose and an interesting pattern of scar-tissue criss-crossing his shaven head. He could see that the man was a skolly, but he warmed towards him, for in Boon he recognised a kindred soul, hooked by the bottle and the wild-weed. Moreover, how many men would buy your clobber, and then generously share the wine bought with your money?

They sat in peace for quite a long time, passing the bottle back and forth and talking in the desultory manner of drunks, while commenting briefly on the leggy girls passing by. They enjoyed the cruel look and obvious disgust of a lady walking her poodle, at which Boon surreptitiously hurled pebbles and ribald remarks: 'Djy met die grys krule en die pretty red bow. Djou ma was 'n skaap en djou pa 'n ou circus aap.. Djy lyk moth-eaten nogal. Sies!'

*Sell his shoes and coat for two bottles of wine

Presently, the passing parade dwindled to the odd straggler going home, and dusk came down upon the park. Boon built a two-out zol of BB tobacco and brown paper check, adding a measure of the wild-weed to give the thing a kick. They passed the zol back and forth, and the pungent blue smoke merged with the evening.

'Djy's 'n lekker pellie, ou Whitey,' said Boon, quite suddenly, displaying a fine set of canines. 'Where you all from?'

It was a good question, and he considered it for some time; but since he had no idea of his whereabouts, and was loath to ask for fear of ridicule, he found it difficult to answer. At length, for the sake of conversation, he explained that he had been born on the sixth day of Christmas in a land beyond the midnight sun.

For a long moment Boon looked at him with his bright, drug-crazy eyes, then smiled slowly and nodded. 'Djar, ek ken die plek, ou Whitey. I know it very well. I was there last Easter; me and ou Lem and the Gympie Street Crew. We smoked a whole arm of boom and drank-out a big can of vlam!'* Giving a sudden sharp laugh and thrusting his evil face close, he added, 'Ek is ook forkkin mal, ou Whitey. Dit lyk vir my die hele blerrie wêreld is mal. Maar mag nie worry, ou pellie blue. Ek is djou pellie.'

In the silence and gloom beneath the trees he felt an unhappy chill of loneliness pass through him, in spite of Boon's affirmation of friendship. The second bottle was empty and the dagga zol was just a slimy half-inch wedge, and ahead of him stretched the long unknown night and whatever was to follow thereafter. He closed his eyes to seek a modicum of peace, a slight release from his loneliness and the embryo of fear in the pit of his stomach. Leaning back against the fence, he allowed his chin to drop on to his chest. Presently his mind began to cloud, and the park and whatever city or town it was in became detached from his existence. A drowsiness crept upon him, which a moment later was black and complete.

ii

He awoke to the touch of hands. His shirt was pulled up to his armpits and Boon was kneeling in front of him, poised for flight, it seemed. The skolly explained sheepishly that he had been examining the shirt and found it such an excellent garment that it was surely worth a bottle of sweetwine, adding that he knew of a place where such a transaction might be made, even at this late hour.

As reality returned, he found that the idea appealed to him; it would be something to do; a form of action. So they set off through the whispering park which was beautiful in the moonlight. All the soft colours, the edgings of the lily-ponds, the blooms and the plinths of the bronze statues, were

*Boom: dagga. Vlam: methylated spirits.

heightened by a light which seemed to come from some inner source, while the trees and the shadows were silent and secretive.

Once again he had the feeling that he had passed this way before. The place was hauntingly familiar. He felt that this silent peace and moonlit beauty, this place with its whispering trees and glowing blooms was his spiritual home. Dropping to his knees on the moist lawn, he spread his arms to embrace it. 'Oh Elysium,' he whispered, much to the consternation of Boon, who was of a much more practical turn of mind.

'We must cut a line, ou Whitey,' the skolly urged. 'The cops sometimes come down here in their patrol-van bothering people like us.'

They hurried on through another square in which there were more lilyponds, a ghostly grey cannon and a hideous bronze work of a departed politician, or deity. A lustrous white building loomed up ahead. Surely the flood-lit palace of some good sultan, he felt. Mounting the steps he bowed before the great doors. 'Salaam!' he cried. 'Salaam, O great one! See your humble subject!'

Boon looked on in drugged and drunken wonder. 'Djy's lekker geaap, ou Whitey; that's only the Art Gallery!'

'Only an art gallery, is it! Anyway, salaam aleikum, o echoing shrine of noble passions!' He trotted away from the Art Gallery, apparently in the right direction, for Boon did not restrain him, and up ahead he saw a long concrete bench set in the wall of the park, screened from vagrant light by tall oak-trees. It was a place of gloomy silence, deserted it seemed. Then he heard the cry of a child: a tiny voice urgent with hunger. Two dark figures came awake on the bench; a man and a woman with alarmed brown faces, null-people, dressed in the rags of abject poverty, who held in tender arms a chocolate morsel. Bowing before the family, he addressed the adults with great respect, for in his mind's sensitized eye he saw a wandering star and a tethered ass. 'No place at any inn!' he cried, nudging Boon. 'We bring not frankincense or myrrh, not even a crumpled brown randtjie or a coin of nickle; but I will sing you a little song:

> Show me the way to go home,
> I'm drunk but I wanna another drink.
> I had a dop of jupe about an hour ago,
> And that's longer than you think!'

Boon laughed loudly in the faces of the hopeless ones. 'This Whitey is lekker psycho,' the skolly said, doing a fair imitation of the ludicrous song-and-dance act.

And to his delight he found that the hopeless ones, though null, were rich in laughter. He did another little dance and grew dizzy, while Boon made the couple a long cigarette, his pink tongue licking along the fat brown tube. Gay farewells were exchanged, and he followed Boon out of the park and into the deserted streets beyond.

They traversed block after midnight silent tenement block, creepy with the lost and wandering thoughts of tenants anciently dead. The shadows deepened and he gripped Boon's arm out of sudden fear, for perched upon a street sign which read 'Skid Row' was a vulture. But on closer inspection it proved to be but a shadow, and the faded sign read 'Glynn Street'. It was a narrow sombre street of crumbling houses, boarded-up against intrusion, but peopled by spectres all around. It stank of violence! They penetrated the gloom, and suddenly he was presented with an incredible sight, for it seemed that a great chunk of the moon had come to earth.

Towering up no more than a mile away, four miles long and half a mile high, it seemed, was a great slab of the lunar surface. It glowed eerily green and a spectral mist swirled about its summit. On one towering edge, beneath a winking green light, stood a spaceship — perhaps a flying-saucer from the star Alderbaran! Taken aback, he cried out in alarm. 'Look Boon! There! A piece of the moon has arrived!'

Boon laughed wildly, the echoes scattering the spectres in the sombre street. 'Djy's forkkin' mal, ou Whitey. That's Table Mountain and the cable station, with the floodlights for the Republic Holiday!'

He gaped from Boon's evil face to the green-glowing mountain, and an ice-cold wind of fear swept through his body. *'Table Mountain?'* Incredible! Only minutes before meeting Boon, he had been sharing a bottle of sweetwine with little Laurie. They had been sitting peacefully on the Donkin Reserve in Port Elizabeth. Holy Jesus, five-hundred miles of space unaccounted for — and how much time? His mind boggled for a moment, then he began to laugh with great inanity and the strange cold wind of fear passed on. He unburdened himself of his shirt and handed it to Boon. 'Here, my friend, take this useless garment. We must celebrate my finest feat of alcoholic teleportation to date. We must have more wine — an intoxicated midnight!'

Boon stowed the shirt beneath his coat, and they walked on through the streets on the edge of the light-spangled, bright-peopled city below. His stockinged-feet were beginning to hurt badly as he followed a few paces behind Boon. The streets and alleys had become dark and twisting, and he knew that they were in District Six. Up ahead the ragged outlines of buildings, ghostly-silent church steeples and the minarets of mosques cut the late-night bottle-green sky. On both sides of the dying streets, humble sleeping dwellings cowered one against the other, awaiting the iron heel of officialdom that would, at length, crush them into the hallowed ground, scattering the voiceless populace across the far Flats wilderness.* At this late hour the solid citizens of the district were in bed, dreaming perhaps of

*Cape Flats Coloured resettlement area

the halcyon days or lying in wakefulness contemplating the uncertain future of their children. Stumbling on towards whatever destination Boon had in mind, in their nocturnal passage, they encountered only the shiftless and the homeless, those twilight souls who wander forever through the hopeless streets of the ghettos of this world.

A terrified cry cut through the bombazine night, and they stopped to meld with a crumbling wall of shadow as a girl raced past, pursued by a dark form with outstretched hands and ill-intent. Within a moment the girl was gone with flying hair, swallowed by the black cotton night. Boon's evil laugh followed the randy hunter and died in the distance with the racing footsteps. And then, further on at a narrow intersection beneath a feeble streetlight, four figures stood dark and tall and motionless.

'I'll talk, ou Whitey,' Boon whispered.

Up in the green-glowing sky the moon moved in and out of the caves of rain, and he felt the first fat drops on his naked back. The magic of the jupe and the boomskuif * was wearing thin. Body and soul were shrivelling. He waited for the directing voice of the kewpie, then the skollies were standing four around him, fingering the buckles of their heavily-studded fighting belts, low on their hips.

'Los hom uit!' Boon said sharpely. 'Die whitey is my ou pellie.'

The four peered closely and the naked violence in the dark faces gave way to a cordial gleam of recognition of a kindred soul: here was no unfortunate stranger lost in the District, to be relieved of his possessions. They began to laugh and gibe in their inimitable way, poking fun at his undressed condition.

'Waar loop djy rond, ou Whitey? Djy lyk lekker ryk, djy met die groot baard, en sonder skoener. Maak 'n las vir 'n dop, ou ryk Whitey!'††

Boon laughed to kill himself, and offered a jovial jab in the ribs as his contribution to the fun. 'I'll get our borrel soetes, ou pellie blue.'††† Then he became another shadow, melding with the night and the District, and was gone forever, and the four gathered around.

'Djy lyk geaap, ou ryk Whitey.' The shaven heads were thrust forward. 'Skyf,' they said. 'Smoke!'

The dagga zol was a three-out zol, and he drew it quick and long into his body. In and out through the convolutions of his brain went the pungent blue smoke, breeding its festering maggots in his mind. The raindrops fell like bright showered jewels in the circle of pale light, and within a minute he was standing tall and dagga-courageous upon a fragile glass pedestal, looking down on the four skollies who, with glinting teeth, bade him farewell.

---

* Dagga-loaded cigarette.

†† Supply the means for a drink.

††† Borrel soetes: Bottle of muscatel.

'Sien djy op die Christmas-tree, ou ryk Whitey.' Their vicious wolf-hounds came out of the shadows and went to heel, and like the girl with the flying hair, they were swallowed by the bombazine night.

The wild-weed zol grew hot at his lips, and he stumbled on down the rain-swept streets of District Six. 'Boon!' he cried in his anguish and loneliness. 'Boon!' And from a hundred sleeping windows came a thousand dark echoes: 'Boon . . . Boon . . . Boon . . . is gone forever!'

The old curiosity-shop was dark and silent. The artefacts upon its verandah cowered like grey and hopeless ghosts in an old mausoleum of the Machine-Age: washing-machines lay dead, their vanquished rotary souls spinning far out beyond Andromeda. Once aloof cool fridges, their entrails scattered to the far ends of the earth, stood agape and stinking. And lonely prams, and wheel-less trikes, their saddles cracked and stiff, never again to feel the human warmth of sweaty little bums. And quiet, unassuming wood and metal things without name. He salaamed solemnly before the ghosts, requesting sanctuary from the driving rain; then he crept in among the mute metal corpses and buried his face in the dust.

iii

In the first dawn, in the grey cradle of creation, a spark was ignited in a lump of smelly protoplasm. For aeons the thing lay unstirring while the world created itself around it. And on the seventh day God, having rested, went away, secretly displeased with the monster of His fashioning, for the thing had acquired delusions of grandeur. Only the voice of the kewpie-doll could be heard in the grey land: 'I'm only kidding; He hasn't really gone away.'

He raised himself on his elbows, and there were the bars — the usual bars — in the wall of the usual police cell. He felt around on the concrete floor for the filthy brown blanket to cover his shivering body. But there were no blankets, nor was the floor concrete: beneath his searching hand he felt splintery, dusty wood.

The grey grew lighter, pearly and distant, and he saw that the bars were not the bars of a cell, but those of a venerable bedhead with brass knobs, leaning against the sagging railing of a verandah. He seemed to be entombed with the strange quiet people of the Machine-Age. Then, quite suddenly a voice came out of the stirring world: from some nearby unseen mosque, came the voice of the muezzin — perhaps a blind one, so beautiful was his call to the people of Islam.

Listening, he closed his eyes to read the darkness, and he saw four men around him, tall and dark, and he heard the echoes beyond the first dawn: 'Boon . . . Boon . . . Boon . . . is gone forever!' Then he remembered the black cotton night and the rain-swept streets of District Six.

The voice of dawn ended on a high trailing note: Allah awaited the veneration of his subjects. Returning to the dust, for he had not the strength to rise, he felt eyes crawling over his face: eyes tickling along on long-lashed legs. Slowly and painfully, for the stiffs had started, the cramps, he inched his head around and he saw the long-lashed eyes: they were wood-smoke grey, and curious, in a beautiful little face of pink-shot alabaster, framed by damp auburn curls: a little boy, hardly two years old. He was clad only in a blue pyjama-top with a white bunny on the pocket. The child squatted on the dusty planks of the verandah, no more than two metres away.

He looked at the little boy and tried to smile, but he knew that it was ugly. And all the while the curious grey eyes studied him silently, for almost a minute, then they seemed to lose interest. The child did a pee, then a little crap, the pink in his chubby cheeks deepening with the strain. The mess was studied carefully and poked with a finger, and then perhaps because of the damp chill of the morning, the little boy moved away and the presence faded.

The alcoholic seizure was complete: he was unable to move. His eyes were fixed on the little boy's turd, at the peak of which a threadworm waved about like a tiny antenna. Presently the worm was joined by a buzzing bluebottle fly. The creature moved with pompous possession over the yellow mess. And then there was another, and yet another. How do they know? Where do they come from? He stared at the busy flies, waiting in fear and revulsion: soon they would have eaten their fill and would find his face; they would move pompously and possessively over his cramp-frozen face, leaving tiny footprints of yellow dung on his lips. In his helplessness he began to weep. Then blessedly, he heard the rustle, and his angel came to cover and protect him with her soft downy wings.

How long had the coma lasted? He did not know. Perhaps an hour had elapsed since the child had done his morning job and gone off to wherever he lived. A damp patch, where someone had cleaned up the mess, was the only evidence that the child really existed. Experimenting with his limbs, he found that the seizure was past, and after a few minutes he crept out from the pile of junk and sat with his back to the wall of the house.

The narrow old street on which the house stood with its shabby neighbours, was splashed by the brightness of the morning sun, and a colourful pageant of cars, carts, lorries and people passed by. They were all Coloured people, and like morning people everywhere there were those who scowled and many who laughed, and a few who wept and lamented.

There were people in rags: scarecrows with hopeless eyes reflecting the poverty of both body and spirit. And there were those who strode in smart business suits. Gay girls who seemed born to laugh, if foolishly, skipped along in pairs and groups. Youths, peacock-proud in sun-bright shirts, walked purposefully about their business. Little boys beladen with copies of the morning papers, their piping voices calling: 'Keep Times, hamburger! Keep Times, hamburger!'* skipped beneath the wheels of urgently hooting motorcars, whose squealing brakes and tyres and cursing drivers added to the morning din of District Six.

The sharp sounds entered his body through a hole in the top of his head, were amplified to a point of agony by his sensitized nervous system and transmitted at peak power along every nerve. He clasped his hands about his head, but the cacophony roared on into his body like an express train entering a tunnel.

Twice he tried to get to his feet, to go off down the street, to find some quiet place to rest, but his legs would hardly support him. He was about to close his eyes in defeat, when a great shadow fell across his body. Raising his eyes, he saw a woman standing over him; a giantess of a woman dressed all in black. The skin of her face was like ancient brown leather beneath a profusion of greying gingery hair. A massive bunch of keys dangled from her girdle. From his cowering position on the floor of the verandah, the woman appeared to be about three feet shorter than the Statue of Liberty.

For about fifteen seconds she stood over him, her motionless jet-black eyes fixed on his face, while she clenched and unclenched her big rough hands, and he felt as vulnerable as a cockroach, though far less nimble. 'So what are you doing on my stoep? Djy met die dirty hairy face, and no shirt or shoes, nogal?' Her voice was as cold and expressionless as her eyes, but she made no move towards him and he felt that the crisis was past; that he was not to be crushed like an insect beneath her massive sandal.

Once again he tried valiantly to get to his feet, but it was hopeless: his knees were like so much jelly; he simply smiled up at the giantess. 'Goodmorning, madam,' he said pleasantly enough, though he was feeling increasingly unpleasant. 'I took shelter from the rain, I think. As you can see. I'm schoonered. Which might suggest that I am something of a bum. In fact I am a wayward seaman. Lady, would you believe that I was a smart young ships' officer before being possessed by the diabolical twins — alcohol and his brother the wild-weed? I am also sorry that I trespassed. I will go away now.'

The clarity of his articulation amazed him, and in spite of the explosions in his head, he grinned. He felt that he handled his case very well.

'Who schoonered you?'

Now, her voice held no menace, had lost its cold edge, and he was happy to find that she understood the things that happen so naturally to a wino. There was perhaps even a hint of compassion in her steady black eyes. And her accent and diction had altered: this was not an uneducated woman, he felt. He began to toy with the idea of asking her if the man of the house might provide him with an old shirt and a pair of shoes, so that he might go

*Cape Times and Die Burger

about his business: The matter was of paramount importance. He must have a drink; alcohol of any kind, in whatever guise, for he knew that within half an hour he would literally be screaming for it.

The giantess did not look like the sort of person who would fall for a straight bite. But perhaps if he explained the position, appealed to the tender maternal instinct which must lie buried beneath her massive bosom, she would come across with the twelve cents he required to purchase a half-jack bottle of meths from the store he could see on the opposite corner, and thus appease his mounting agony. The process of gathering his mental resources was in itself pure agony, and he achieved only a modicum of success as he gazed across the narrow, downward sloping street. The old single and double storeyed buildings, some broad, others narrow and not quite perpendicular, were shabby relics of Cape Town's past, their dun-coloured fronts briefly glorified by the brightness of the morning sunlight and the laundering they had received from the rain. Directly opposite, two young Malay women were choosing fruit from a hawker's barrow, while the man's ancient cry: 'Lekker tamaties, drie vir a bob, ek sê,' was delivered in a stentorian voice that would carry to the most distant hovel in the yards behind the buildings.

With the harsh cry of the hawker reverberating painfully inside his skull, he returned his gaze to the giantess, who was toying with some coins in the pocket of her apron, and regarding him with a hint of amusement in her eyes. 'Who schoonered him?' Well he would tell the truth. He had not the mental energy to fabricate a likely story — a plausible yarn of how he had been robbed. 'Nobody schoonered me,' he said firmly. 'There was this fellow I met in the Botanical Gardens. I gave him my shirt and we came up here to get a bottle of wine. On the way up we met some other fellows, and Boon . . .!'

'Ha Boon! That Boon! That skolly! You're lucky you've still got your jeans and socks.' The giantess gave a great bark of a laugh which boomed in his head and scattered his painfully assembled thoughts. Then she turned away towards the front door of the house, and it seemed to him that all was lost: he was finished, doomed to slink away down the street, to bum a few coins, to find a smokkelhuis and buy a bottle of cloudy shebeen wine — or to be picked up by a patrol-van, to die the 'littledeath' in the cells on the upper floor of Caledon Square Police Station.

The activity in the street was increasing. Within his line of vision, ragged spindly-legged children, their high sweet voices ringing to the house tops, gleefully scattered trash in the gutter, while bigger boys with an abundance of morning energy bounced balls against walls and careered down the street in rickety soap-box carts. Little girls skipped, played at pretty ladies or huddled in giggling conclave. From upper windows, angry mothers screamed at the boys with their dirty balls. rescued washing from makeshift lines, exchanged the time of the day with their neighbours and bemoaned in loud voices for all to hear, the laziness and wine-bibbing of some of their men. Tired and ancient men came out to sit on the pavement on homemade stools, to thaw their night-stiffened legs: while at the entrance of an evil-looking alley, a bunch of skollies stood talking, their scarred heads wreathed in blue dagga smoke. He noticed that his wayward friend Boon was not amongst them.

'Whitey.'

The giantess was standing in the doorway of her house, and he looked at her with just the faintest of hopes rising in his breast.

'You don't look so good, witman. You'd better come in off the stoep for a while. Corpses are not uncommon in the gutters of District Six, but a white one might raise some embárrassing questions!' She turned abruptly, followed her great shadow into the house, and was gone.

Sanctuary!

For a whole disbelieving minute he sat with his head hanging down between his knees, then reaction set in and his body began to pulsate, and suddenly he had the full rattles, every nerve shrieking for the release that only alcohol could bring. During this supreme agony, two young men came out of the house to look at him. He gave them his ugly smile and tried to still his rattling as the young men walked around him, viewing him from different angles and positions, as if trying to decide what manner of animal he was. They were nice looking fellows, well-groomed and dressed in expensive shirts and trousers. In a slow, dim way he learned that their names were Willy and Eddie and that the giantess was their 'mommy': Mommy Stilhuis. Willy, perhaps twenty years old, had blue eyes and light skin and the gingery hair of his mother, while Eddie, a few years younger, was dark-complexioned and had beautiful black hair reaching almost his shoulders.

'You seem to be suffering, ou Whitey,' Eddie said in an amused off-hand sort of way. 'Maggy Aap's piss. I suppose. That's a bad smokkie. They never wash their bottles.'

Willy bent over and peered closer, shaking his head slowly and clicking his tongue in mock compassion. 'Such a bab-a-laas,' he said, drawing the word out slowly and whispering in Eddie's ear. The brothers nudged each other and burst out laughing. 'Come inside,' Willy added quite seriously. 'My mommy will give you some of the blood of that dog that bit you last night. So you were with Boon, ne - - - shoo!' Once more the brothers nudged each other in a knowing way, then they took hold of his arms and raised him to his feet, so that he stood with his back supported by the wall, while some mad monster beat him on the head with a mallet. The noise of

District Six receded, then came rushing back with renewed violence. But he managed to remain vertical, though he swayed like a reed in the wind. As he followed the boys into the house he felt vaguely that he had ass's ears.

iv

La Residence Stilhuis was leviathan in character. Beyond the long, narrow throat of the passage, it widened to a voorkamer almost the size — and furnished in the manner — of a small hotel lounge in Victorian Bombay. Dark cabinets, richly glowing with polish, stood against walls behung with bright tapestries depicting unlikely elephants and tigers sewn on a background of violently green eastern jungles. There were brass gongs in blackwood frames, while bright slip-rugs covered the highly polished floor. Two exquisite Bali heads adorned a massive blackwood dresser, upon which was arranged a lovely collection of Royal Doulton plate. On the walls were heavily-framed prints of royal people long since dead. In the centre of the room, draped by a green-baize, tasselled cloth, was a grand-father of a table with heavily carved legs. There were Swedish oak couches with foam-rubber cushions, and a radiogram the size of a coffin. And on a shelf running around the walls were knick-knacks to make the mind boggle. It was a hideous, overpowering, museum-like room, and he saw it all in a kind of dark agony of impatience, for there was not a functional bottle of liquor in sight!

The rattles had settled down to a steady tremble and the occasional epileptic jerk. His head felt like a baked pomegranate, the brain cells rattling around like dry seeds in his shrivelled skull. His body was as cold as the coldest day in the middle of the Ice-Age, and the stinking wine-sweat trickled down his sides.

Eddie put a record on the 'gram, and the big room vibrated with the high-wattage, stereophonic twanging of a million guitars, while an inhuman voice shrieked out the story of a lover who had jumped, fallen, or been pushed off the Tallahasse Bridge; it was not clear which, but his nerves shrieked in unison with the singer. A great fear came upon him, for he was sure that he had seen a bushy tail slipping behind one of the cabinets in a darker corner of the room. In anguish, he turned his eyes upon Mommy Stilhuis who was seated at the big table. And perhaps she saw the plea, or was aware of the mounting madness of his withdrawal.

The giantess screamed at Eddie to turn the volume down, and the voice of the singing girl trailed off like the cry of a tortured soul descending into a medieval hell. 'Take him out to the yard and let him wash his filthy face,' Mommy said to no one in particular. Then, his curious arrival on her 'stoep' apparently forgotten, the giant woman began to sort and count the pile of coin and crumpled notes which lay before her on the table, and make entries in a cash book.

Eddie smiled at him, delighted, it seemed, to be of service. He followed the lad down a short passage to a spotless kitchen where an elderly woman was decanting wine from a six-bottle can into a row of sparkling pint bottles, while a second old woman capped them and wrapped them in newspaper. Several full cans of wine stood on the floor. It was an unbelievable sight! And then he saw the massive linen-cupboard which stood against one wall. Its doors were open, and its tiers of shelves, neatly packed with fresh linen, stood at an odd angle to the frame. In the false back were rows of sealed bottles of assorted liquor. Had he not been feeling so crook, so very near the end, he would have been elated; nevertheless he was amazed. In his travels over the seas of the world in merchant ships, he had come across some very cunning illegal dives, but La Residence Stilhuis put them all to shame. It was a lulu of a shebeen — a jolly old smokkelhuis of five-star rating! He had been invited into a veritable land of milk and honey! The ugly opulence of the voorkamer, the false-front of heaped junk on the verandah, and Mommy's tough, worldly manner, were no longer a mystery to him.

Beyond the kitchen lay a courtyard with a dusty ashy floor: an awful dirty place, littered with decaying junk and surrounded on three sides by hovel-like rooms with rusty tin roofs. The doors were peeling, ill-fitting and sagging, and many windows held no glass. There was a strong smell of drains and an atmosphere of poverty in the sad drab yard of Mommy's tenants. Beyond the buckled roofs, the green and silver minaret of a mosque sparkled in the morning sunlight. And towering up, as old as time itself, was the brooding, misty bulk of Table Mountain. Down in the bay, beyond the beautiful city and the harbour, the ships lay like coracles on some tranquil pond.

The old people sitting outside their rooms in the free and unrestricted sunlight gazed at him across an unbridgeable gulf. Their eyes were mute, dull and without hope. And to several children in their ragged clothes who came to form a ring around him, to gaze up at him in wonder with their beautiful big brown eyes, realisation was yet to reach out its cold, unfeeling hand. He became suddenly conscious of some deep, sad thing within him, something that had nothing to do with his maudlin state of mind. The emotion was an amalgam of shame and guilt: the shame of what he had become, and stinging guilt for squandering the rights and privileges that these old people had never had.

Curbing the grief that he felt, he smiled at the children, who turned shyly away, to continue with their games, to live the moment on hand in the shadow of the mountain, beneath the wonderfully blue canopy of the Cape sky.

Eddie touched him on the shoulder and showed him a stand-pipe with a tap on top. Stripping off his jeans, he sat beneath it clad only in his socks and bright-blue skants. Eddie opened the tap and the water gushed out, creating a pain where the jet struck the top of his head. Much to the amusement of the children, he coughed and snorted like some mad beast, and when he could stand it no longer, he crawled out from beneath the tap and sat on the rickety bench in the sun. Slowly and without control, his head drooped between his knees, and he began the peaceful drift away from reality into the black void of amnesia.

2

i

'Suig djy nog, ou Whitey?'

The voice was distant and unfamiliar. He brushed away the unreal cobwebs shrouding his mind, and listened. But it was not the voice of the kewpie: there were other sounds, growing in intensity, and he knew that he had returned to his empty world of reality. How long had he been away this time — a millennium? He lifted his head, and there stood a boy with a towel in his hand. The figure became familiar. It was Eddie. And what did Eddie have in his other hand? Could it be a glass of cold back tea? Eddie was smiling broadly as one who comes bearing a gift, holding the glass out and inclining his head towards it in encouragement.

He smelt the raw brandy and his guts heaved and twisted and he felt the bile rising, while the moist beads of revulsion stood out on his brow and his mind screamed with compulsive desire for the alcohol. Like a suppliant at an altar, he reached out with both hands and took the glass, resting it on his knees, where it trembled as the spasms racked his body. With Eddie's help he lifted the glass to his mouth, all the while retching and hawking. He choked on the first gulp, but a little of the neat spirit entered his stomach, where it was most unwelcome and quickly rejected. He clamped his teeth tightly but the brandy mixed with bile was forced through his lips by the power of the stomach's rejection. Eddie wiped his face and he took another swig, which stayed down, glowing like molten metal in the pit of his stomach then spreading its magic fire throughout his blood-stream.

'There, it's all over now,' he said, smiling foolishly at Eddie. Looking around the yard with new interest, he found the children and the old people were watching him warily, as if expecting some new madness from this half-naked white man. All that he could offer them in the way of further entertainment was a heavy belch as he polished off the brandy. Then he smiled and waved his hand — everybody's rubicund uncle!

Now that his body and mind were appeased, he was able to have a gallant conversation, about nothing in particular, with a little chocolate-coloured girl dressed in baggy blue shorts and a vest, who said that her name was Cookie . . . 'and why does Oom take his pants off . . . sis!' Which reminded him of his undressed condition, which seemed unimportant on such a fine morning and in such good company.

Regrettably, the glass was empty, and he handed it to Eddie, who looked at him with sleepy amusement. 'Is djy nou reg, ou Whitey?' The boy laughed and flicked him in the face with the towel. 'My mommy say do you wanna eat?'

The very idea was appalling! He explained the delicate condition of his stomach, his digestive tract and withered taste-buds. 'Perhaps a little later, Eddie. My sincere thanks to your mommy.'

He found that he could stand, and had hardly donned his jeans when a young woman came out of the house, and stood looking over towards him. She held a child which looked very familiar. And he remembered the old curiosity-shop and the quiet people of the Machine-Age and bluebottle flies.

The girl spoke to an old woman sitting in the sun outside the kitchen door, and then she came sauntering across, and he saw that the child on her arm was indeed his little friend of the early-morn turd. But now, dressed in his blue rompers and shirt and tiny white shoes and socks, the little boy was fit to put on a Christmas-tree. The child twirled a tiny finger in his brushed, deep auburn curls, all the while regarding the world with his curious wood-smoke grey eyes.

The great slug of neat brandy was whirling in his brain. He felt seven-feet tall and as handsome as the very devil as he bowed before the girl, looking at her closely. Now here was something that old Vladimir T. had been trying for ages to convey on his canvas — this sloe-eyed beauty! Her skin was like honey-coloured satin, dusted by the Hand of God with the same brush that He uses for the petals of the wild roses of the Cape. Her hair — as black and shiny as Eddie's — was drawn back from her brow and secured with some scarlet notion at the nape of her graceful neck. The sunlight shimmered on her floral slax-suit and glinted on her gilded sandals as she moved her feet. Reluctantly, he dragged his eyes away, and looked at the child.

'Top o' the morning, Matie,' he said, taking a tiny hand and shaking it in a formal manner. 'I trust that you've finished crapping for a while? And what might the name be, Captain?'

'He's Binty,' said the girl, smiling at the child, who wore a perplexed frown.

'Binty! Well . . . now, that's a fine name! And you're his mother . . . and your name will be something like . . .' He felt his etheric body moving out of the perpendicular, to the right. Ever so slowly, his spirit began to cant away, almost out of control. Tiny flames of fear and panic flickered in his heart, and then with an effort he brought his parts together again . . . 'and you'll have a lovely name like Razeel or Fatima?'

The smile had faded from the girl's face. She looked at him nervously. 'You'd better sit down again,' she said quickly.'You nearly fell over just now. Djy's lekker geaap, ou Whitey.' Then she giggled. 'And you look so funny. No shoes; just socks, jeans and tattoos. And a beard and a gold ear-ring; just like a pirate. I'm not Razeel or Fatima . . .'

'She's Gertie!' cried Eddie, flicking at her bottom with the towel. 'Flirty Gertie!'

The girl rounded on the laughing, wary boy. 'Hou djou bek, djou vark!' she spat. A gold sandal lashed out at Eddie, but she missed him as he side-stepped and went off, flicking at the scattering, laughing children. Embarrassment and temper had brought a high colour to the girl's cheeks. She looked up at him and the smile slowly returned. 'Yes, I'm Gertie,' she said in a coy delightful way, canting her head. 'Gertie Smit.'

He stared at the girl in mock disbelief. 'Gertie. This beauty?' he soliloquized, waxing wistful and gazing up at old Tafelberg, dressed in his morning coat of bright misty mauve and green. 'Gertie. What an incredible thing. Henceforth you shall be Manya; and remind me to tell you about my Manya in Singapore: she of the lotus blossoms.' Thoughtfully, he returned his gaze to the mountain and time spun backwards and froze. Sharply etched against the North Face of Table Mountain was Singapore's towering Cathay Building. He became conscious of a curious eastern fragrance and the tinkle of temple bells, woven into the coarse fabric of sounds and smells arising from beyond the tin walls of the yard. Momentarily, he was relieved of the tarnished middle years of life and he felt the bubbling expectant buoyancy of youth in pursuit of a pretty girl. And then someone struck him in the temple with an ice-pick. He closed his eyes against the blinding pain shooting through his head, but within a moment it was gone, and he looked at Manya, who seemed to have missed his moment of agony. Fun and bewilderment chased each other across her beautiful almond eyes, then she looked around the interested group that had gathered.

Willy was there now, and a surly skolly, wearing a great black-and-white checked cap, pulled low over his receding brow. He wore skin-tight jeans and a filthy roll-neck jersey. Ou Lem, they called him, and his taciturn presence seemed to cast a cold dark shadow across the sunlit yard.

Manya's wandering gaze returned, the questioning expression in her eyes suggesting that she was prepared for anything from this strange, tattooed, bearded creature which had appeared out of the night. 'You're mad, ou Whitey. I'm just Gertie. But Manya is a beautiful name. Perhaps I'll keep it while you're here.'

The half-tumbler of neat brandy cruising through his system had reached peak-power. Adopting a mock-serious mien, he took the girl's hand and brushed her fingers with his lips. 'Oh, well,' he said gallantly. 'Gertie is as good a name as any. By the way! What is a name, a creed or race? In the final analysis, it is the purity of the heart and spirit that counts. My name is Paul, and I am so very glad to meet you; glad to know you all; delighted to be in this pleasant place!'

Manya retrieved her hand, and then seemed undecided what to do with it. At length, she averted her eyes and fussed unnecessarily with Binty's hair. 'I must be going soon,' she said. 'Will you hold him while I fetch my bag?'

'Why, surely!' He took the child and held him in an unpractised way. At first Binty protested mildly, then settled down in the crook of his arm, examining him closely with those curious smokey-grey eyes. 'I hope that we're going to be friends, matie,' he chuckled, gobbling at the tiny fist which had become entangled in his beard. The child's eyes widened, then he smiled, and his bell-like laughter rang around the drab yard.

The brothers, seemingly bored with the proceedings, began to chaff Manya in the light-hearted manner of young Coloured people: 'Koop 'n hemp en skoene vir djou man, Gertie!' cried Willy, ducking away as the girl made a dive for him. 'Sy's Manya!' shrilled Eddie. 'Manya, koop 'n borrel dop vir djou whitey. Hy suig nog!' The pair fled towards the kitchen door, laughing and taunting, with Manya in hot pursuit. They disappeared through the doorway, and there were shrieks and scuffling sounds from within, then silence as Mommy's terrible voice carried out to the yard: 'Bly stil, djulle! Die Whitey is babalaas. Los hom uit!'

Ou Lem, the skolly, looked him over coldly and with much disapproval, and the scarred, ugly face reflected the malevolence of his thoughts. Quite suddenly, ou Lem smiled in a tight-lipped way, then with a contemptuous spit, the skolly moved off towards the kitchen, and the sunlight glinted ominously on the brutal studs of his broad fighting belt.

ii

With the departure of the young people, even ou Lem, he felt somewhat lonely. A few yards away, Cookie played at hop-scotch, her bare feet sending up little puffs of grey dust. The old people had lost interest in him, and were going about the slow, interminable chores of old people. The women swept endlessly in front of the doorways of the rooms, shuffled back and forth to the tap, to the kitchen, carrying small basins of washing and crockery. They emptied coffee pots across the yard, and shuffled off to the toilet, to empty slop-pails. The men scratched and scraped at the bowls of ancient pipes, spat, looked up at the mountain. And in the rooms, in the gloom, the shadowy movements of the old people were slow and monotonous in the twilight of their lives.

The euphoria created by the brandy was beginning to abate. Seating himself on the bench, he settled Binty on his lap and gazed about this strange shore upon which the tide of wine had cast him. He felt quite philosophical about it: life had dumped him in this place; why not linger awhile? After all there was nowhere else to go. He was fully aware of the fact that the mood that was upon him, and the state of well-being, would not last much longer. Time was not static; soon the pendulum of his life would start to swing again in one direction or the other: either he would get drunk to a point of amnesia, and forget for a while, or he would sink into that awful state of withdrawal and nervous anxiety which follows a prolonged bender: slinking along the pavements, avoiding the eyes of sober citizens, starting in fear at his own shadow, and finally, seeking out like an animal a place to crawl into to hide from the ugly world and await the onset of the horries.

Quite suddenly, his mind side-tracked away from the gloomy thoughts, and he experienced a spell of mild schizophrenia: a portion of his mind occupying itself with the contemplation of Mommy's linen cupboard, while the romantic cells of his brain considered the image of the sun-splashed girl who had disappeared into the house a few minutes ago. 'Damn!' he said, grinning sheepishly at Binty, who was watching a white ship of a cloud sailing across the impeccable sky. 'What an annoying and puerile thing is this romantic heart of mine!' And it had plagued him from an early age. Ever since — following some long-forgotten impulse — he had kissed a black-haired poppet on the verandah of a holiday boarding-house in Durban, he had had a desire to flirt with every pretty girl he saw, to toy with the soft hair around her ears. 'Silly bugger,' he mused. He laughed softly and bounced Binty on his knee. But the image of Manya refused to dissolve. The picture seemed to sharpen, and soon took precedence over the tantalizing vision of the rows of liquor bottles in the fake cupboard. For a while he indulged in a happy little fantasy: a few brief moments of warmth in the contemplation of the sunny friendly girl with the dimpled smile. But happiness, however brief, was not his lot or gift, and soon his mind was clouded by a premonition of pain and grief. A chill of apprehension passed through him, leaving a feeling of hopeless melancholy, followed by an upsurge of unhappy memories: a recollection of shattered dreams and withered aspirations, unrequited love and broken promises. This was not a new experience. Time out of number the ghosts returned from those departed days when drinking had been a pleasure, to move wraith-like through his alcoholic mind, to point jeering fingers at his cold and lonely soul. But he accepted the fact that the 'days of wine and roses' were beyond recall and that all he had left now, were the thorns.

Binty wriggled from his knee, and he held the little boy between his thighs to keep him away from the filthy grey dust of the yard. He hoped that Manya would soon return, and perhaps bring a cigarette. The shadow of gloom was passing, and in the warmth of the sun he was feeling as physically well as could be expected. The sporadic sharp pains in his head had abated, and there was only a dull throb at the base of his skull.

He was kept amused by the quaint propriety with which Binty acknowledged the waves and greetings of some of the people who entered the yard by the creaky old back gate. The child gravely nodded his head and raised an index finger to those who called his name on their way to the kitchen to buy their morning wine: the old babalaasdop, the hair of the dog.

Binty had discovered the ludicrous ear-ring: a little gold circlet, a relic of a boastful bet on shore-leave in Hong Kong, and was plucking at it with his tiny fingers. And then Cookie came up to sit beside him, humming a little tune and kicking at the dust with her horny, bare feet. She told him that she made up her own songs, but though he listened attentively he could make nothing of her talent. Her backyard idiom was beyond his experience. But she had a sweet little voice and perfect pitch. Examining his ear-ring, she said that she would make up a song about it.

Then Manya came out of the house, swinging her bag and blowing out a great cloud of cigarette-smoke.

He stood and greeted her gallantly with his ugly smile. 'Here, sit on the bench and tell me your dreams and aspirations!' His voice sounded over-loud and theatrical, and he felt that to bow again would be over-playing the part. He sat down again and beamed up at the girl, admiring the deep spots of colour in her cheeks and the way she canted her head slightly when she smiled.

'Okay,' she said, seating herself tentatively on the other end of the bench. 'But only for a minute. I must go to work to-day. We don't usually work Saturdays, but we're behind with winter orders.'

'It's *Saturday?'* The bright figure of the girl dimmed and distorted, like a reflection in ripple glass, and momentarily he closed his eyes. Not only had he travelled almost five hundred miles, but he had been a whole week at it, for he recalled quite distinctly that it had been a Sunday morning that he and little Laurie had spent on the Donkin in Port Elizabeth.

'Yes, it's Saturday, Whitey. Saturday twenty-ninth May nineteen-sixty-nine.' There was a perplexed frown on Manya's face. 'You looked funny just then, Whitey. Are you still feeling bad?'

'Why . . . not really. It . . . er . . . it's just that I hadn't realised that it was Saturday, that's all. May I have one of your cigarettes?'

For a further long moment, she sat quite still, regarding him with thoughtful concern, then with a trivial shrug of her slim shoulders, she dismissed whatever it was that was on her mind, and reaching in her bag she brought to light a cigarette packet and a box of matches, and put them in his hand. 'There are a few in there that you can have. I'll get another packet on my way down.'

He lit a cigarette and looked up from the dying match, to surprise a curious expression on the girl's face. It was fleeting to be sure, but he knew that he had seen it: a shadow of concern in her eyes. Then a quick smile shaped her lips and she stood up, slinging her bag on her arm. She gathered Binty up and settled him on her hip. 'I must be off now,' she said.

'Does the child go to work with you?' He took Binty's little hand and gave it a shake.

'I leave him with people in Woodstock. He gets filthy in this yard and he frets in the house.' She smiled in her soft, warm way. 'Good-bye, Whitey. I hope all goes well with you.'

A little sensation of panic and loss urged him to reach out and touch her cheek, but he desisted. 'Will I see you again, Manya?'

'It'll be six o'clock before I get home. You'll be gone by that time. But perhaps I'll see you again sometime.' She seemed to hesitate before turning away, as if she had something else on her mind, then with a final quick, bright smile she went across the yard and out of the gate.

3

i

The junk-strewn yard was deserted beneath the ten o'clock sun. The children were not to be seen, and all the old people were in their rooms. The back gate remained closed, for there was a lull in the smokkeling business. By this time the legal bottle-stores would be open, and the 'mailers' — the runners from shebeens big and small — would be at the counters, buying supplies for the long-week-end thirst.

He leaned back against the tin fence. The sun felt good on his bare torso, but he lacked the simple contentment of smoking a cigarette in a quiet yard in the sun. Over and above the ever-present anxiety about some unknown thing, he was disturbed by the fleeting expression he had caught in Manya's eyes. He tried to analyse it, but all sorts of impressions and stray thoughts side-tracked him. Eventually, he tried to shut his mind completely — dead ship. But this was a mistake. The kaleidoscopic fragments of light behind his closed eyelids were far more disturbing, and his body began to jangle like a sack of cow-bells strung from his mind. The effects of the brandy had worn off, and he was desperate for a drink to settle his nerves again.

But even the acquisition of a bottle of jupe was far beyond his means. He looked towards the kitchen, hoping to catch sight of Willy or Eddie, but in the kitchen there was only an old woman scrubbing a table. He fingered his ear-ring, but the act brought neither inspiration nor hope, for who would want to buy such a cheap little thing? To put a straight bite on Mommy Stilhuis might work, but probably wouldn't. Like all shebeen-keepers she was necessarily tough and unbending. The drink he had been given earlier, was only meant to set him topside-up, and see him on the way. While considering the price of a bottle of wine, a strange thought struck him. The fifty cents required might just as well have been fifty rand. There was an almost audible 'click' in his head. It was as if some chemical cell in the brain-complex had been waiting patiently for the word 'rand' to appear, for quite suddenly he remembered the roll of fifty he had locked in a suitcase — somewhere. But though he strained away at the idea, the whereabouts of the suitcase eluded him completely. After a while, his headache increased, and he tossed the suitcase with its unlikely fifty rand on the fantasy scrapheap.

Cookie came out of the house and sat down beside him. She was nursing a naked rag-doll with a time-ravaged, waxen face and lank black hair. The little girl sat crooning softly to the unfortunate thing, assuring it of her love, and reminding it that when they 'got big' they were going to sing together on the bioscope.

Listening to Cookie's prattle he felt almost child-like himself, and he experienced a certain empathy. Presently, assisted by the drowsy warmth of the sun, the lack of nourishment and Cookie's crooning, he drifted away from the drab yard with its sad-life old people, into a hazy world without time, in which he spent most of his waking hours, these days. Cookie's little voice drew faraway, disembodied, like the voices heard through the thin, scabby walls of the old rooms in which he had lived and made love, had the horries, and dreamed of ancient lives and places down the fabric of time.

Pulling his mind back from its disjointed wanderings, he tried seriously to reconstruct the week of oblivion that had passed since he had paid-off the coaster in East London, but he experienced only a frightful pack of mental nonsense — then blank! Perhaps there was no past at all? Perhaps he had come suddenly into being, swirled out of a wine-bottle like a djinn, in the park of the giant rodents? Maybe the fragmentary pictures that he called his memory were only an illusion?

Then he discovered the suitcase again: a dull green fibre suitcase, and he knew very well that he had bought it in Singapore, in one of the little junk-shops which line teeming Southbridge Road. He saw the thing clearly. It had become a very battered suitcase, he recalled, for it was some years ago that he had last visited the Lion City. The suitcase and its point of origin in the past, was beginning to stir vague memories. But no sooner had he grasped them, when they slipped away again, for a common suitcase and a distant eastern seaport are flimsy data upon which to try to base recall of the pieces that go missing out of a drunk's life.

The atmospheric crackling in his mind eased off, and his body, though weak, hardly trembled at all. Experience had taught him to be very wary of such periods of respite. He re-lit the cigarette-butt, and while idly watching Cookie running a comb through the doll's coarse black hair, he was suddenly presented with a picture of the contents of his suitcase. He saw clearly the faded blue suit, and there were a few sets of clean jeans and frayed shirts, underwear and an alarmclock known as 'the liar'. There was a yellow plastic box of toilet gear and a creased envelope containing such documents as a seaman needs. There was a blue, Gideon Bible and a book of poems by Dylan Thomas — which he had half-inched from the Seaman's Mission in Sydney, Australia — a collection of the shorter works of Jack London — complete with the stamp of the Natal Provincial Library — which he had purchased from a bum in the bar of the old Anchor Hotel on Durban's waterfront — the gloomy old back bar where once a seaman from a cattle boat, an intense, unhappy young man named Eugene O'Neill had tarried for a while during his 'Long Day's Journey Into Night'.

And there was not much more in his suitcase, for the gathering of property, however 'portable' had always eluded him. But of the whereabouts of the suitcase, he was now certain: he had left it in the baggage-office on East London Station—nine hundred miles up the line! And he found little solace in the knowledge that without the presentation of a ticket, the suitcase would remain there for three months, as safe as if it were in the vault of the South African Reserve Bank. Scratching around in the hip pocket of his jeans he found the little buff-coloured ticket. It had had a rough passage, and was barely legible, but he was delighted to see it, for it gave credence to the existence of his suitcase.

As wary as he had been of the period of respite, he was quite unprepared for the sudden shrinking of his consciousness: that strange sensation of being imprisoned within the shell of his own body, looking out at the world through two tiny round holes, which were his eyes. In abject fear his being huddled back within the dark reaches of the shell, and there was the very real wish that he would die at that moment, depart from the world of reality with its suffering and injustice.

Then gradually his dissolving world solidified. Cookie was singing 'Raindrops are falling on my bed'. The little girl explained that she sang it this way because there was a bad leak in the roof above her bed, and when it rained Mommy had to put a basin there.

He gave up the foolish occupation of trying to reconstruct the blank week, of how he had arrived in Cape Town and what had happened in between. He was here, and that was that. It was much easier just to lean back against the fence and close his eyes.

ii

When he awoke, the sun was quite high in the morning sky, and there was a little old man squatting before him; a little gnome of a man, whose face was the colour and texture of an ageing apricot. He had quick hazel eyes and a toothless grin which threatened to sever his jaw from his upper face.

Staring at the gnome for a long moment, he tried to fit him into the phantasmagoria that the shallow, uneasy sleep had produced in his mind. Then he realised that the little man was actually there before him, in the sun-splashed yard of La Residence Stilhuis.

The gnome wore a white waiter's jacket with 'Fred's Chicken Grill' stitched in red above the pocket, and on his head sat a maroon fez at a roguish angle. 'Morning, basie,' said the little man, his quick simian eyes alight with intelligent interest. He took a green serviette package from his pocket and handed it to Cookie, who began to dole out the broken biscuits to the other children who came running from the rooms. 'I bring the biscuits from the kafee,' the gnome continued, adopting an expansive manner. 'They don't mind if I take them. Sometime there are pies, too. And even chickens that are left over. The larnie at the kafee is a good man — a Portjie.'

He was fully awake now, and the sleep in the sun had not improved matters at all. He had a slug of water from the standpipe and rinsed his mouth out. 'It is good of the Portjie to let you have the leftovers,' he said, returning to the bench. 'It is a pity that you don't work in a bottle-store or a bar.'

'Ha!' the old man exclaimed, slapping his knee. 'I did once work in a bar. But there they guard the stuff like gold. To steal a chicken is nothing. To steal a bottle of brandy from a bar is tronk business. Anyway it is better to steal food for the children. In District Six they buy enough wine and stuff every week-end to float a ship.' The old man produced a shiny tin of makings, and began to build a dagga zol. 'Basie is a matroos.' It was a statement rather than a question.

'Yes, I am a seaman. How did you guess?'

'You have a good beard; not a thin thing like the young goats in the city wear. And you have pictures of sailing ships and women on your arms. I am called Achmet Smit,' he added somewhat irrelevantly. 'The child that I saw you holding this morning is my grandson.' He gave the brownpaper zol a good lick, then ran on: 'I was once a matroos. A cook in the old days on the railway ships, on the *Erica,* that used to go to Australia for timber and railway sleepers, and carry coal on this coast.' He lit the zol and the pungent blue smoke drifted lazily above his head. After a couple of thoughtful pulls, he passed the zol across. 'Hy's nie rooibaard, ou matroos, maar hy skop.'

Now here was an unexpected break! Gratefully he drew the smoke into his lungs, savouring the wild taste of it in his mouth, and a minute later, the enjoyment of the singing lifting of his mood of depression. It was a pretty potent zol, right enough. 'Hy's nie rooibaard, Achmet Smit,' he laughed. 'Maar hy skop lekker!'

The old back gate creaked open, and two ragged men came into the yard. They carried a Singer sewing-machine, a piece of rope wound around the handle of the familiar old fashioned plywood cover, so that each had an end and they carried it quite easily between them, though they looked groggy and badly in need of a drink. Inwardly he commiserated with them, for he understood exactly how they felt. They nodded to Achmet Smit as they passed, and then continued on towards the kitchen door, through which they disappeared.

'They might get a six-bottle can of sweetwine for it,' Achmet Smit observed, without real interest. 'Mommy Stilhuis will hide it away in her cellar with the . . . er . . . other property, and then when things have quietened down she'll sell it on the Grand Parade for fifteen or twenty rand.'

Watching the blue smoke drifting across the yard, he recalled the old curiosity-shop with its relics of the Machine-Age, and he wondered who had carried the washing-machine in, and what sort of deal he had got. He was struck by a sudden notion that suffering drunks develop almost miraculous powers: they seem capable of changing almost anything into wine.

'Your son, the father of Binty, does he work in the city?' It was a patently sly and rather stupid question, and having voiced it, he was immediately sorry and angry with himself for his mean prying. Reason told him that there was nothing more behind Manya's friendliness and kindness than the desire to help him: that old-world characteristic which he believed the Coloured people to still retain: the genuine, spontaneous sympathy for any person, of any race, who is ill or needy. Other than the enigmatic expression he had seen in her eyes, there had been nothing of the old 'come on' in her attitude. But despite reason, he felt somewhat like a fish that has caught sight of a colourful lure, and is waiting around for it to reappear.

The old man's eyes were a little bemused. The corners of his long lips lifted almost imperceptibly in the hint of a smile, as if he had noticed the transparency of the question. 'I have no son,' he said simply. 'There was once a son, but he died a long, long time ago. His mother also died at about that time. Then I took another woman.' He nodded towards one of the rooms, where a thin, middle-aged woman was standing in the doorway. She stood there for a moment, looking across towards the bench, then aware perhaps that she was the subject of the conversation she moved away out of sight. 'She is also ill,' Achmet Smit continued, gently tapping his own thin chest. 'Chest trouble.' He was silent for a moment, then he smiled mysteriously. 'The girl you were talking with this morning is our daughter.'

Startled, he groped frantically for words. 'The people here have been very kind to me,' he said hastily, generalizing in an effort to side-track the old man away from any idea he might have of pursuing the subject of Manya. 'In a little while, I must go. But I hope to come back again some day.' And this was true enough. With the edge of the mounting horries blunted by the powerful dagga cigarette, and his mind more or less at ease, he saw clearly that he must leave La Residence Stilhuis. Recalling the earlier premonition, he knew that to linger and get drunk again would only precipitate an even uglier situation from which might arise a great deal of grief and unhappiness for others.

For some minutes, in that part of his mind concerned with such matters, the nucleus of a vague plan had been forming. He felt sure that he could raise at least a shirt from Willy, who was the broader of the two boys. He would then make his way to Sea Point and find a sheltered spot on the sands under the Promenade, and there he would sleep and drink water. In the evening, when the beach was quiet, he would have a naked swim. He would suffer, of this he was certain, but he would throw off this drunk he was on! And later on when he was rested, he would make his way to the Coaster Berth in the Victoria Basin. There, he felt sure, he would be able to raise a pair of shoes from the Zulu crewmen, some food and maybe a rand or two to see him on his way back to East London, where he could pick up his suitcase, for without his documents he had no hope of getting another job. It was as easy as that! He felt very pleased with himself — *resolute!* He was moving in a positive direction. Just a little farewell drink now, from somewhere, and he would go and find Willy.

The two sewing-machine merchants came out of the kitchen, closely followed by ou Lem. True to Achmet Smit's prediction, the one had a paper carrier which obviously held a six-bottle can of wine. His companion, with great volubility, was warning him not to drop it, and what would happen to him if he did. Then they joked a little and smiled happily in anticipation. But not for long!

Abreast of the bench, ou Lem caught hold of the wine-carrier's arm and pointed to the glass jar. 'Maak hom oop!' the skolly snarled. The wine-carrier stood stock-still for a moment, then he lowered the bag and held it between his feet, gazing in silent apprehension, first at ou Lem's vicious face, and then at his companion, who was bigger and not quite so afraid, it seemed. 'Ag nay, ou Lem!' the man shrilled. 'Ons het 'n groot crew daar by ons plek!'

Beneath the vast cap ou Lem's baleful eyes swivelled up to the face of the man who had spoken. The skolly took a step forward and his hand slid into the hip pocket of his jeans, where, for sure, there was a three-star jack-knife. 'Maak hom *oop,* djou *dief!*' Out came the knife, and with the quickness and agility of a cat, ou Lem stooped, slashed the carrier from top to bottom, and was back erect, the point of the knife an inch away from the wine-carrier's throat. 'Is djy doof, vark?' The skolly's face was tight with violence.

The wine-carrier, his face blotchy-grey with fear, eased away from the knife-point, then stooping, he lifted the can and broke the seal.

Laughing evilly, ou Lem pocketed his knife. He screwed the cap off and tossed it to the ground, then with the can in the crook of his practised arm he put the neck between his blubbery lips and took a vast swallow, his Adam's apple working up and down his scrawny neck, while twin streams of sweetwine ran down his chin. For a good ten seconds the skolly drank, then wiping his hand across his mouth, he handed the can back. 'Der, vat djou kannetjie, djou forkkin' gemors!' he snapped.

Without bothering about the cap, the can in one hand and the ripped carrier-bag in the other, and with his companion bringing up hurriedly in the rear, the unfortunate wine-carrier scurried fearfully out through the back gate. Ou Lem's cackling, evil laugh followed them, then the skolly turned slowly towards the bench, the eyes beneath the vast overhang of his cap shining with violence as he unbuckled his belt. It slithered out of the loops of his jeans, and in a flash he had hold of the tongue-end, swishing it about behind him, for all the world like an angry cat flicking its tail. Now, with the bright buckle of the belt describing sparkling arcs above his head, ou Lem advanced on the bench. 'Swish! Swish! Swish!' sang the belt — then Mommy's terrible voice cut across the yard.

'Lem!'

He found that somehow he had arrived on his feet, leastways he was standing behind the bench. The interesting incident of the wine-jacking had occupied his attention to such an extent that ou Lem's intended attack on him found him breathless with surprise and fear. It was unbelievable! Now he stood waiting and watchful. Other than run to the house, there was little he could do to protect himself against a man armed with a knife and a heavy belt.

At the sound of Mommy's trumpet-like call, ou Lem stopped in his tracks. The skolly stood glaring, and lashing ineffectually at the air with his furious belt. Achmet Smit sat as if frozen to the bench, and Cookie had her knuckles to her mouth and was whimpering out of fear. After a great deal of staring and lashing about with his belt, ou Lem buckled it back on, then he cleared his throat and spat upon the ground a great slimy, wine-flecked oyster. 'Ek sal djou *kry,* witvark,' he hissed, then he sauntered off towards the kitchen.

He looked down at the filthy gob near his feet, furious about the insult it implied and his inability to do anything about it. A flush of hot anger rose to his face and he jumped over the bench, then stumbled as one of his knees buckled. *'Bastard!'* he shouted in impotent rage. *'That gob is the best part of you, ou Lem!'* He stood trembling and waiting, but the skolly only looked over his shoulder and continued on towards the kitchen.

He hung his head for a moment, feeling beaten and sick and ashamed, then he turned towards the bench. Cookie looked up at him with her big moist eyes, and he patted the little girl's silky black head. She sniffed and wiped her nose on the grubby back of her rag doll, then the incident apparently forgotten, skipped off into the one of the rooms.

Achmet Smit stood up and touched him on the arm. 'Watch hom, ou matroos,' he whispered. 'Watch that skolly. Ou Lem is mad in the head from too much dagga and vlam. He thinks that every white man is a policeman and against him.' The old man smiled apologetically. 'I am sorry that that happened. Now . . . er . . . I have something for us. Would you like some . . . er . . . soetes, ou Matroos?'

iii

Achmet Smit's room was like a thousand others in the backyards of District Six, a simple square box, shabbily furnished. It was clean and tidy, but it stank of poverty: a cloying dank smell compounded of oil-stoves and stale food, old clothes, sweat and bedbugs, an atmosphere thoroughly permeated by the hopeless vibrations and thoughts of a hundred years of struggling humans.

The woman, far older than she appeared to be from across the yard, sat on a Globe chair at a small deal table. She was thin and hollow-cheeked, with a bald patch in the centre of her sparse grey hair. The skin of her face was taut, and carried a criss-cross pattern of fine lines, like ancient yellow porcelain. Looking at her in the half-light of the shack, he found it difficult to accept that this wan creature was the mother of the delectable Manya.

The woman nodded a brief greeting, then stood up and shuffled across to the sagging double bed, to pick up a tiny brown infant which was rapidly winding up to squall force. Soothing the baby, the old woman sat down on the bed and began softly to hum a lullaby.

'The child belongs to one of the younger women who goes out to work,' Achmet Smit explained. The old man fetched a half-full, three-bottle can of sweet wine from a wardrobe and filled two enamel mugs. Indicating the chair vacated by the woman, he pulled another up for himself. 'What will you do to-day, ou matroos? Will you go back to your ship?' the old man asked after about five minutes of silence during which time they had each drunk half a mug of wine.

He told the old man the awful truth, and it seemed to amuse him very much, for he laughed and slapped his knee in his manner, nodding across at the woman, urging her to join in the fun. But she seemed indifferent, even to life itself.

'So your things are in East London and you are here in Cape Town without money and clothes.' Achmet Smit's eyes were alight with the adventure of it all. 'Man, I wish I was young again and still a matroos! I tell you, I would set the world on fire! I remember the old days when we paid-off after an Australian trip. Man, the wine flowed like a river in District Six! And the girls came from as far as Paarl to be with us. It is so long ago that I can hardly remember it all.' He topped up the mugs and then sat staring into space, as if drifting down all the years to those carefree days.

Sighing with weariness, Achmet Smit's woman lay down beside the child, and she began to cough the sobbing, choking cough of the consumptive. Disturbed, the tiny infant waved its little arms about and then settled down again, fragile and innocent.

The old man looked at him gravely for a moment, then his eyes slid away to the woman on the bed. 'It is her chest,' he explained again. 'The District

Nurse is coming to-day to take her away.' Achmet Smit's eyes lingered on the crumpled figure of his woman, then he leaned closer. 'I'll be glad when she is in some place where they look after people like her,' he whispered. 'She keeps me awake in the night with her coughing. And sometimes I can't get up in the morning when I'm on early shift at the kafee. She has been with me for a long time now, but I will be glad when she's gone. I can't take it any more.' His eyes grew moist and distant and he nodded his head, silently pleading for understanding. 'You know what I mean, ou matroos, né?'

'That child ought not to be in here,' he said, somewhat lamely, for he could find nothing else to say.

'True, but the woman pays her a rand a week to look after the child. Things are hard, ou matroos. The Portjie pays me only five rands a week to clean up his place. It is a struggle to live these days.'

'What about the girl — your daughter; will she look after you?'

'Gertie?' The old man shrugged and emptied the last of the wine into the mugs. 'You know what the young are like. They sometimes forget where the food came from when they were small. Gertie lives in the house. She has a nice room in there; and her own bathroom, nogal! She earns good money at the clothing factory and she does help me out a little. I don't pull on her life. There is the child that has no father; but who am I to say anything about that: these things happen. I think that she is yust an ordinary girl: a little bit of hell and a little bit of heaven. But she looks well after the child; not like some around here who yust let their kids run wild and turn into skollies. And she looks well after Cookie, who is nobody's child.'

'Cookie?'

'She came here one day a couple of years ago when she was yust a little thing as thin as a match, and hardly any clothes on her back. Mommy Stilhuis spoke to the authorities, but no-one could find out where she came from. Cookie sleeps with Mommy in the big room in the house, and Gertie buys her clothes, and sees to it that she doesn't run wild. Soon Cookie will be going to school — that Gertie of mine is a great one for schools and learning. Already she has taught Cookie how to read; and here am I, over sixty, and I have to make a cross for my name!' As if the last statement had triggered a new line of thought, the old man brightened perceptibly. But there is no need to worry about me, ou matroos. Soon I'll be getting a pension — from the government, nogal! Mommy and Gertie fixed it for me. You see I was in the *war!*'

The woman began a new bout of painful coughing, and draining his mug he stood up. 'Let us leave your woman in peace,' he said, walking to the door.

Achmet Smit followed him out of the room, and at that moment in different parts of the city tens of thousands of pigeons rose into the sky, and a milli-second later came the crack of the noonday gun on Signal Hill.

'The twelve o'clock gun!' Achmet Smit said in a fair panic. 'I did not think it was so late. I must be at the kafee now. *Magtig!*' The old fellow stood in his peculiar way, bowed at the knees, his hands and skinny wrists dangling from the sleeves of his white jacket, his manner altogether apologetic, as if his imminent departure for the café were something of a vast breach of etiquette. 'Ou matroos will still be here to-night?' He nodded hopefully, his face split by his alarmingly wide grin. 'Perhaps we can talk some more about the sea?'

He took the creased old brown hand and shook his head. 'No, Achmet Smit. But I will come and see you at the café before I leave Cape Town. But if I can't make it, I hope all goes well with you.'

The old man nodded eagerly. 'Yes, you must come and see me at the kafee. I will fix you up with a chicken.' He drew himself up and cut a smart salute. 'Totsiens, ou matroos. Loop lekker vandag, en pasop vir ou Lem en sy pellies.' Achmet turned away and hurried back to his room; perhaps to bid his woman a final farewell.

4

i

The yard of La Residence Stilhuis was deserted beneath the noon-day sun, but he could hear the prattling voices of the children coming from one of the rooms. He crossed towards the house, to seek out Willy and beg a shirt. He felt both mentally and physically foul: heavy sweetwine is the world's worst hangover cure! He was neither relieved of his morning condition, nor drunk. Rather, he was in that gap of almost clinical insanity which exists between the tapering-off of one prolonged bender and the beginning of the next. However tender and sore his feet were, he was still *resolute,* and eager to be away. Ou Lem's crazy enmity was disturbing. He was not a fighter, nor was he in any physical condition to defend himself against an armed and vicious skolly.

He had almost reached the kitchen door, when Willy himself appeared. The young man's face was set and purposeful, and he hurried past without a look or a word. Sprinting across the yard, Willy secured the back gate with its big bolt, then he disappeared into the first room at that end of the yard.

Sensing something untoward in connection with the smokkeling business, he waited for Willy to reappear. But after five minutes, there was still no sign of the young man. His feet were now so sore that he longed to sit down, and after waiting for a further minute or so, he sidled past an old woman who had appeared in the doorway, and entered the house. It was only after he had passed through the kitchen — through a ghastly miasma of food smells rising from the shiny pots on the range — that he realised what Willy's panic was about, and that standing in the doorway of the voorkamer of La Residence Stilhuis was not the best place for him to be in his disturbed state of mind, unshod, shirtless and half-drunk! He also knew that to retreat to the sancturary of Achmet Smit's room was out of the question, for two gentlemen in the voorkamer — otherwise occupied by Mommy, Eddie and ou Lem — had seen him, were in fact looking at him as though he were a big steaming turd standing there. He remained rooted in the doorway, trying to fashion a casually disinterested expression on his slack face.

Eddie was fiddling with the knobs of the radiogram — which was mercifully silent — while ou Lem, seated on the edge of one of the many couches, cracked his fingers soundlessly in agitation. The skolly still wore his vast cap, but not in the usual fore-and-aft manner. It lay in the athwartship position, the peak pulled down over his starboard ear. Ou Lem seemed to find something of great interest in a picture on the opposite wall, for his eyes remained intently fixed upon it. Mommy Stilhuis was seated at the big table. Her back was towards him, but he felt somehow that the giantess was aware of his presence.

Feeling idiotically theatrical, and torn between the desire to flee, and yet to know the meaning of the solemn assembly, he folded his arms modestly across his chest and faced the gentleman in the dark suit who was standing at the other end of the big table. The man had the cunning sallow face, the pencil-line moustache and the gleaming wavy black hair of the stereotype Lothario that excites the otherwise prosaic dreams of backveld farm-girls. Also, this fox-faced gent might just as well have had CID stamped across his brow in big black letters.

The second visitor was a Coloured gentleman. He stood beside the doorway of the front passage, leaning indolently against the wall, one highly-polished Chelsea boot crossed over the other. He wore a bronze time-to-shine suit and a tie of no earthly pattern. There was a soft, indulgent smile on his heavy sensual lips, and his eyes were sleepily hooded as he gazed across the length of the room.

'Come in,' Fox-face said at length, smiling coldly, 'Make yourself by the house.'

Feeling all eyes upon him, he walked slowly into the voorkamer. Seating himself next to ou Lem, he joined the skolly in silent contemplation of a large photograph of a particularly flinty-looking Smuts, attired in his best civilian bib-and-tucker. After a moment, he glanced at Mommy, who was wearing a ridiculously tiny pair of steel-rimmed spectacles, through which she was studying a post-card-size photograph. She glanced over the top of it and gave him a sour look.

The scene was distorting curiously at the edge of his vision, as though the room were being bent and curved to fit into a sphere. He glanced quickly from one cop to the other: neither was looking at him. In a panic, he closed his eyes to shut out the shrinking world; but this was a mistake, for he was conscious of being tipped upside-down and whirled about something awful. And then there was a voice, speaking as if from a great distance: a flat, emotionless voice.

'He is a dangerous man. He was seen in this street last night.'

Opening his eyes, he found that nobody in particular was looking at him. The room had reverted to its true oblong shape and old Fox-face was pointing to the photograph in Mommy's hand. 'We want him for questioning in connection with a stabbing which took place last night near the Seven Steps,' Fox-face added, his manner cold and arrogant. He clearly saw himself as a big-wheel in the field of criminal investigation.

'I have never seen him before in my life,' Mommy said, flipping the photograph across the table. 'And why do you come to my house?'

The detective's face grew bleak. It was an ugly face, without the least vestige of sensitivity. For a long moment the flat black eyes regarded Mommy with the intensity of a snake confronting a field-mouse. But the giant madame of La Residence Stilhuis was quite unmouse-like. She sat there, returning the poisonous stare, but with a hint of amusement in her own black eyes. 'Well, sir?' she urged lightly.

'We know you. We know that you smokkel here!' the cop snapped, at length. 'We know that these skolly bastards gather here and buy wine!' He picked up the photograph and flicked at it angrily. 'One of these days I'll catch you at it, old woman!'

Mommy Stilhuis gave a short bark of a laugh and turned to Willy, who had come into the room. 'Fetch some glasses,' she said sharply. 'And bring that small can of Skip — the one I bought last week.' She turned to the detective. 'Sit, meneer. Have a glass of sherry and tell us some more about this man in the photo. After all, it is so unusual for someone to be stabbed in District Six, that we must keep an eye open for him.'

'I am on duty, and this is not a matter for jokes,' Fox-face snapped, pulling out a chair and seating himself. He glanced at his comrade, who was still smiling faintly; then his eyes moved to Eddie. 'Have *you* seen this man?'

Eddie took the photograph and studied it for a long while, his young face unnaturally blank. He held the photograph close, and then at arms-length, then he went to a window for better light, and stood there, rubbing his chin, while a freezing silence settled on the room, and Willy came back and placed a three-bottle can on the table. He polished two glasses with a snowy tea-cloth and poured a good shot into each, placing one at the elbow of Fox-face and handing the other to old smiler, who drained the glass at a swig and handed it back without thanks.

'I don't know him,' Eddie said. 'But I've seen him around. The last time was about a month ago.'

He found that the voorkamer was beginning to shrink again, and the temperature was rising. The desire for air and space was almost overwhelming, but he fought against the yearning to rush into the yard, for he knew that he would be called back. His head was throbbing and spongy, and the stinking sweat was beginning to run down his sides. He looked at the can of cheap dark sherry, wondering if he would get a turn; and ou Lem was leaning forward somewhat eagerly.

The detective's eyes lingered on Eddie's innocent face, then he picked up his glass and swirled the sherry a little, his own face tense and thoughtful. Finally, he drank his sherry and returned the glass to the table. Willy refilled it, but the cop quickly raised his hand. 'Enough thank you,' he said firmly, looking from face to face. 'Now you people must realise that this is a serious business. A man has been murdered, and I intend to catch the killer.' He stood up and took the photograph from Eddie's fingers, then he swung on ou Lem. 'En jy!' he barked. 'Don't tell me that *you* don't know this vark!'

The detective at the doorway was staring at the skolly and he was no longer smiling. Ou Lem took the post-card and looked from one cop to the other. He slewed his cap fore-and-aft, and then glanced at the photograph. 'Ya, ek ken hom,' he said flatly. 'We was in the tronk by Wellington last year, but I doesn't know where's he now.'

'Djy lieg, djou vark!' The Coloured cop moved quickly across the room and stood over ou Lem. Snatching the great cap from his head, he beat him across the face with it. 'Ons ken djulle was gister saam gewees. *Waar's die hond?*' He stood back waiting, and looking at ou Lem as if he would be delighted to punch him in the face. Finally, he flung the cap down, and turned towards Mommy, as if about to speak, but he was forestalled.

'He was not with anyone yesterday!' Mommy's great voice filled the room. 'He does my floors every Friday. He never moved out of this house from morning till night.'

The plot was thickening, he thought. He wished to Christ that Willy would give him a drink, for the voorkamer and everything in it was becoming vaguely detached, like a stage setting. Without knowing how it had arrived there, he found quite suddenly that he had the photograph in his hand, and that Fox-face was watching him closely. His turn had come. But he was in no frame of mind to care about it, one way or the other. He had not committed a crime; certainly he had never stabbed a man. He understood something of the skolly element—the cross which the Coloured people had to bear. But he was no skolly, and he was not even interested in the photograph—until he looked at it. It was perhaps five to seven years old and showed a smiling young man with hope and dignity in his face. The young man had thick neatly-brushed hair, and was smartly dressed in a light suit. The face was very familiar, and when full realisation dawned, he was thankful for the slack, unresponsive muscles of his face and his wine-dimmed eyes, for they were unable to express the surprise that he felt. More than ever now, did he need a drink, and he found that, either by chance or design, Willy had come between him and the cops, and was holding out a full tumbler of sherry. He made short work of it, and Willy took the glass and moved aside, while he had another good look at the photograph. And he recalled Mommy's words when she had found him on her stoep that morning: 'Huh, Boon! That Boon! THAT SKOLLY! He looked on the reverse side of the post-card. 'Boonzaier, John'. The name was type-written, followed by a series of dates and code numbers.

Surprise had untangled the skein of dull half-thoughts in his mind, dispelled the cobwebby figments. He saw again the evil face of Boon in the pale gleam cast by the street light on the corner, and he heard the evil laugh following the dying footsteps of the racing girl and the randy hunter. That face bore hardly any resemblance to the young John Boonzaier of the photograph. Ah, Boon, he thought sadly, what have the intervening years done to us? To me, born with a silver spoon in my mouth, who was offered every opportunity: an expensive education, complete with straw-basher and gold-striped tie, and was found wanting? And to you, who walked in youthful dignity and confidence, yet received only the crumbs from the table of society, which have turned to wormwood in your mouth? A dark shadow of pain crossed his mind. He closed his eyes briefly, then flipped the photograph to the table. The surprise had passed, and he managed to bring old Fox-face into focus.

'En jy, witman?' the cop snapped. 'What are you doing in a shebeen, with Coloureds?' There was a nasty inflexion in the voice, which suggested that by associating with these people he had let the side down, as it were.

'I was caught in the rain,' he said, truthfully enough.

The detective seemed astonished, and raised his eyebrows. 'It's not raining; it's a *fine* day!'

'It was last night, when I came up here,' he said, feeling foolishly trapped, for he knew what was coming next.

'And what were you doing up here, walking about in the rain at night? Do you want your throat cut; or are you so well known in this shithole that you are safe?' Suddenly, feeling perhaps that he might be on to something, Fox-face pointed to the photograph. 'Do you know this man?'

It was a direct question, to which there was only one of two answers: 'yes' or 'no'. How easily booze leads one into unsought trouble: first Manya, then ou Lem's crap, and now this. He wanted to walk away; he wanted simply to get up and walk out of the house and down the back lane, to make his way to Sea Point, to the cool sand beneath the Promenade, to bury his face in the soft sand and sleep forever!

'Well, do you know him?'

'I don't know anyone in this town. I'm from East London. I walked up here last night quite by chance. I have certainly never seen this young man in the photograph.' At best it was a half-truth. At its worst it was withholding information from the police, whose job was already difficult enough. Avoiding the detective's eye, he wondered just how far down the scale of decency and righteousness he would slide.

For a long moment Fox-face fixed him with his poisonous stare, then he snatched up the photograph and slipped it between the pages of his note-book. 'So you're a dronklap from East London,' he said sourly. 'Perhaps you'd better go back that way, mister. We have enough hoboes down here.' Once again he looked at each person in the room in turn, then he picked up the can of sherry and studied it. 'No supplier's label,' he said, his eyes fixed on Mommy's face.

The giantess shrugged. 'Perhaps they forgot to put one on; or maybe it just came off somewhere,' she smiled.

'It was washed off!' snapped Fox-face. 'Then this can was filled from a big jar.' He put the can back on the table and pointed a long finger in Mommy's face. 'Ek sal jou kry, ouvrou!'

Suddenly it was all over. With a curt nod at Mommy, Fox-face walked down the front passage, followed by his comrade-in-arms. Eddie saw them to the front door, and returned, quietly smiling. 'Fork hulle,' he said, without malice. Putting a record on the gram, he screwed the volume up to a maddening jumble of sound. His mother yelled at him to turn it down, and the sweet gentle voice of a girl emerged from the cacophony.

A reaction of general relief followed the departure of the police. With her great bunch of keys jangling at her girdle, Mommy lumbered off to the kitchen. 'Whitey,' she said over her shoulder, 'remind me to get some labels printed for my bottles; must conform to the law, you know.' She chuckled, and then yelled at Willy to go and open the back gate. 'Someone is knocking it down, by the sound of it. Some babalaas vark, I suppose.'

Once his mother was out of sight, Willy quickly filled the two tumblers, and then headed for the kitchen. 'Catch another dop ou Whitey. Catch a luck, ou Lem,' he said over his shoulder, departing with the half-empty can.

Ou Lem seemed to have lost some of his enmity. The skolly downed his sherry at a gulp, and then laughed, displaying a fine set of canines, but no other teeth. When some palaeontologist of the future discovers ou Lem's wedge-shaped skull, he will jump for joy, and call it *Oulemmus Regionis Sextae,* or something like that, and the astonished world will learn that the *Missing Link* has at last been found. Doing a little jig, the skolly picked up his great checked cap and went off into the kitchen.

The second tumbler of harsh, carbide-tasting sherry put paid to his mood of dejection and self-revulsion. If Boon had indeed stabbed a man to death, the police would eventually get the skolly, without the practically useless snippet of information he had to offer. Looking down the passage, he saw Willy talking to his mother, and he had the feeling that there was something of importance he had to ask the young man, but he could not think what it was. Indeed, he was feeling peculiar in more ways than one. His physical vision had cleared miraculously. Looking around the big room with its agglomeration of knick-knacks, drapes and pictures, he thought that it was exotic beyond compare. The Bali heads, and even old Smuts seemed to be smiling. He found, too, that he had to concentrate deeply to recall who he was, and even so he was not sure if he was right. But it was of no consequence in such a delightful place. Feeling somewhat like a fledgling angel, he went through the kitchen and followed Willy out to the yard.

The day was hot and still up on the slopes, without the vestige of a breeze; but the mighty throbbing pulse of the Mother City beat on: a dull vibration rather than an actual, definite sound of ten thousand internal-combustion engines belching their filth into the static air. And from beyond the corrugated-iron fence of La Residence Stilhuis came the rising voice of Saturday District Six.

5

i

The hammering on the gate continued unabated, and Willy hurriedly drew the great bolt and flung the gate wide open, to admit a remarkable-looking couple of men.

Fairly stunned by the incongruity of the newcomers, he stood a few paces apart from Willy as the first man passed him by: a Merchant Navy officer! A four-ringed captain of a ship in full uniform of immaculate blues and gold-braid, the impeccable cap tilted at just the right angle. He seemed a man in his early forties, with a neatly-trimmed gingery beard. The man's eyes were blue and clear and apparently unseeing, for he walked on across the yard and disappeared through the kitchen doorway without looking to either port or starboard. So quickly had the officer appeared, then vanished, that he might have been merely a vision. Since Willy seemed not in any way perturbed, he assumed that the captain was one of Mommy's superior customers.

Not since he had last read his boyhood illustrated copy of *Treasure Island,* had he seen anything resembling the second man, if a human being it was! The thing was skinny in the extreme, covered by a filthy-grey garment which might once have been a safari-suit. The spindly bowed legs, grey with dirt to the calves, terminated root-like in a pair of crumbling sandals. From the midst of a tangled bush of dirty grey coir, a pair of mad black eyes glared around the yard, then darted at Willy. And the thing spoke:

'Avast, ye young vark! Keep a drinking man out, will ye!'

It was a strident voice, which might have been trained in a tall-rigged ship, and Willy stepped back as the thing's attitude became threatening.

'The police were in the house, Uncle Ben,' Willy explained, his face sullen. 'They have just gone away.'

'The boere, eh. Ought to have raked 'em with shot and shell, sir!' A mad laugh rang around the yard, and the incredible creature moved away. 'Repelled 'em, did ye! Ha! Weel, I'm off to splice the fucking main-brace, and eat some cheese!'

A strange sensation of schizoid unreality forced him to close his eyes, and for a moment he felt quite sober, then his mind went off at a strange, questioning tangent: *Ben? Avast? Cheese? Are there other invisible worlds existing in parallel to our biosphere? Is it possible that there is no such a thing as fiction? Do the characters which we readily assume are the creations of the fertile minds of writers such as Robert Louis Stevenson, in fact really exist in some other time-phase, using the minds of such writers to slip across the border, as it were, to wander around forever in the world of mortals?* No! This was madness! He opened his eyes. Ben Gunn was on his way across the yard. The old drunk had a knapsack, and it obviously contained an empty six-bottle wine-can, for the glass neck was sticking out of the ripped side.

Blinking, he turned to Willy. '*Who* is that?'

'Ben I dunno who,' Willy said. 'He gets a pension from the Royal Navy. He comes here every month at pension time and drinks himself drunk. Then he goes away again till next pension time. My daddy used to know him a long time ago in the war.' Willy scowled. 'He gives us a hard time. My mommy says that he has hollow legs: he can drink-out a six-bottle jar at one go.'

Ben Gunn had disappeared into the kitchen, and from his mind, but the nagging familiarity of the captain's face urged him to go back into the house and make the man's acquaintance. The more he thought about it the more familiar the officer's face became, until he was convinced that he knew him. But how did he know the man; how could he know such a fine, upstanding man with such a clean cut of jib? Perhaps he had sailed under him as a cadet? No, that was impossible; they were of an age. He blinked and strained away at his crumbling mind; then he had it! Of course, the man was the split image of a long since deceased uncle, whose picture used to hang in the family house in Durban. Well now . . . that would be a suitable coincidence with which to open the conversation. Squaring his shoulders, he took a few steps towards the house; then reason struck! How filthy you look! What would the man think of you, a drunken scrounging, half-dressed 'bo? His shoulders slumped and he turned sadly away from the house and watched Willy take a great brass padlock off the door of the room nearest the gate. It was the room into which the young man had gone when the police arrived. He walked up and peered into its gloomy interior.

'Is djy nog hier, ou Whitey?' said a voice from the gloom.

He stepped into the foul-smelling, dagga-reeking room, and looked about. The room contained nothing but a sagging old bed and mattress, and reclining upon it was his wayward friend Boon. A filthy blood-stained cloth was wound around the skolly's left hand, and his clothing was splattered with brown blood-specks. On the floor, beside the bed, was a three-bottle can with a finger of jupe in it. Boon was merrily drunk.

'Ek het djou borrel soetes, ou pellie,' Boon said, nodding eagerly and smiling his evil smile, so different from that of John Boonzaier. The skolly reached behind the bed and produced a dark bottle. 'Dé, ou Whitey,' he said proudly.

Accepting the bottle, he experienced a glowing sensation of power: the bottle he was holding was actually his; he was a man of property! He admired it for a moment, then broke the seal and poured a good quarter of the heavy sweetwine into his stomach, where it burst into flame on contact with the rest of the junk in that long-suffering organ. A sort of phlogiston was generated in his mortal engine, and his temples throbbed with the pressure of his over-heated blood.

Boon sat up and unwound the crude bandage. Holding up his palm, he exhibited a long, shallow gash. 'Sea Point varke,' he said, grinning. 'Ek het een van hulle dood gekap!' He went on to explain how a bunch of skollies in a car, apparently from Sea Point, had attempted to take the bottle from him, outside the shebeen by the Seven Steps. He had stabbed one of them in the neck and run away. 'Ou Lem sê die hond is waar dood,' the skolly added.

With growing apprehension, he listened to the tale of Boon's flight through the night, pursued by the stabbed man's maddened companions, and it occurred to him that old Fox-face was certainly quick on the uptake. The wine-induced heat of his body was being rapidly dissipated by a chilly psychic wind which sprang from some unknown source in the region of his heart. As his brain cooled, the full realisation of what Boon had done struck him like a physical blow. This man sitting on the bed, smiling his evil smile, had actually stabbed a fellow human being to death for the sake of a bottle of cheap wine, which he did not even own! *'Oh what havoc wreaks the innocent grape!'* A strange sound, which he classified as the maniacal cackle of the spotted hyena, escaped his lips, startled ou Lem, who had appeared in the doorway. Taking another long swig, he passed the bottle to ou Lem, who had been eyeing it appealingly. The skolly took a long pull, and offered the bottle back. But he shook his head. He found that he had no further desire to drink warm sweetwine in the stinking atmosphere of the room with its violent vibrations. The urge to take great gulps of sweet mountain air was powerfully compelling. Ou Lem shrugged and carried the bottle to the bed, seating himself next to Boon. With their heads together, the skollies began to discuss the visit of the police, and what course of action should be taken to evade old Fox-face who was, apparently, an implacable hunter.

He listened for a while, but then a singing, swirling mistiness engulfed the room. The voices of the two skollies receded rapidly. Panic-stricken and gasping for breath, he groped his way towards the bright rectangle of the doorway — and hurled! A thick jet of liver-coloured liquid shot from his mouth, spraying the dusty earthen floor of the yard. With the early afternoon sun grilling his head, he leaned against the back fence, while his heart pounded away and his guts twisted in agony. After an age, it seemed, the pain and the nausea subsided. He waved a farewell of sorts to the two dim figures in the room, then staggered to the stand-pipe, the water from which was cool and sweet as he washed his mouth and allowed a little to trickle into his aching stomach. For many minutes he sat on the bench in utter weariness and total dejection, drifting slowly away from reality to a point of suspension between the heaven of oblivion and the hell of consciousness: the limbo of the drunk. And he wondered vaguely which would be his ultimate destination?

He was soon to know.

A cool dark shadow fell across his body, bringing blessed relief from the grilling sun. He raised his head, and he saw standing there, a few paces away, the giant black figure of Mommy Stilhuis. She looked into his eyes with an uncomfortable intensity, as if seeking to see beyond them, into his very brain, while her own black orbs were inscrutable, reflecting only the minor surface details of his figure and the bench. For some fifteen seconds she looked at him; then she said:

'A few years ago a man like you came here, Whitey. Perhaps he was an older man, but like you, he drank too much and ate too little, and he died in that room where Boon is. Nobody killed him, he just died. He coughed up his liver and was finished. I had a lot of trouble with the authorities. Like you, he was a man who ought never to drink at all. Believe me, I know what liquor and wine can do to some men. And you're one of those men, Whitey. This is no place for you. I can see that you are not trash, and I'm not running a benevolent society, but I would like to help you.'

Once again he felt the chilly psychic wind. The cold sweat stood out in little globules on his bare torso and he stank of the wine-sweat and the filthy spew, and he was hardly able to think at all for the fear that was upon him, but he got the message. 'I'll go away now,' he said with an effort. The words were a taunting echo of those he had spoken that very morning on the verandah. Or was it yesterday morning, or the day before? He did not know. 'Perhaps Willy will give me an old shirt, shoes are not so important, and then I will go away.'

'And if you had a shirt and shoes, where would you go, witman?' The black eyes twinkled briefly with amusement. 'If you managed to get through the day in your condition, without being picked up, tonight you would be crazy for a drink. Then the shoes would go, then the shirt, and you would be back to square-one. No, Whitey, you'll not go away yet. I was never a person to feed anyone into a police cell. First you'll eat and sleep, and then you'll eat again; and then we'll talk about shoes and shirts, and perhaps a couple of rands. *Come!*'

Meekly, almost puppy-like, he followed Mommy to the kitchen. His soul was in a bad state of erosion. He felt that the grey light in the kitchen ought to be brighter than it was, for sunlight shone through the doorway and filtered through the red-and-white checked curtains at the window. Seating himself where indicated at the table, he caught sight of a movement in the gloom of the passage, and he choked back the cry that rose to his throat, for in the deep gloom of the passage stood the spectral figure of an old man with a bushy head and mad black eyes. In a moment, the spectre was gone. Briefly he closed his eyes, then with all the will-power at his command — which was not very much — he addressed the plate of steaming stew that an old woman had placed before him. It seemed, thereafter, that he was engaged in the most titanic battle of his entire life. His throat was constricted, his taste-buds unresponsive, his mouth seemed to be full of steaming blotting-paper. But he fought on, watched by the two old women and the silent figure of Mommy Stilhuis. Little by little, occupying aeons of time, it seemed, he managed to get the tasteless mass into his raw stomach. Then there was a glass of cold milk and the terrible battle was over. But how bloated he was! Painfully, he arose from the table and bowed to his silent retainers. He felt that he ought to make a speech of thanks, but then Eddie had him by the arm.

'Kom, ou Whitey.'

The boy steadied him, and guided him out to the yard. The sun seemed enormously hot, and his body pulsated with the heat generated by the food. Holding on to Eddie, he dragged his heavy body across the yard, not knowing, or caring at all, where he was going. And then Cookie came up and took his other hand, and it seemed that his destination was the room where Boon was hiding. But the skollies were no longer there. At the door, Cookie let go of his hand. The little girl stood back, nervously nibbling at her thumb-nail. Her great brown eyes were child-bright, but old with the wisdom of the gutters of District Six. In his maudlin state of mind he felt a great out-flowing of love for her in her simplicity and wisdom.

'Sleep in here for a while,' Eddie said. 'I'll put the lock on the door and nobody will worry you.' The boy picked up Boon's empty can and went out, returning a few minutes later with the washed can half-full of water.

The stench and the heat in the corrugated-iron box were awful. It was like a Cretan goat-shed. He slumped on to the sagging bed, his head dropping out of control on to his chest. Eddie put the can down beside the bed and then went out and closed the door, and within a few minutes the room was like a sauna-cabinet. Without bothering to get up, he poured some of the water over his head; it was almost as warm as the sweat running down his body. But in spite of the great discomfort of the heat and the awful, bloated feeling of his body, he soon felt himself losing his tenuous grip on consciousness. He lay down on the mattress, still damp from Boon's occupation, and presently the great black beast of sleep pounced upon him.

ii

'Because of the imbalance created in the brain in particular, and the system in general, by the secretion of a toxic acetaldahyde, manufactured by freak enzymes in his mysterious liver, the disturbed mind-psyche of the chronic alcoholic is in constant conflict with reality, to a lesser or greater degree . . .'

He lay in a veritable bath of perspiration. Never in all his life, had he felt so filthy! By some form of osmosis, perhaps, the stench of the room seemed to have found its way under his skin. The physical horror of it was far more disturbing than the voice in his head. The voice was like that of an old friend, like the kewpie-doll. He was unperturbed by it; he had heard it a dozen times since his discharge from the State Hospital. He knew that he had only to open his eyes and he would see her standing there: Doctor Milly Mayhew, reading the 'Riot Act' to the recovering alcoholic in the drying-out ward. But he did not feel like opening his eyes. He had heard it so many times in the past that he knew the 'Riot Act' by heart.

'. . . the hallucinations, some benign, others horrifying, experienced by the withdrawing alcoholic, are due mainly to his weakened and devitaminized physical condition. The motion of the brain is set in reverse: instead of thinking rationally, it un-thinks, as it were. In this vulnerable condition, the objective mind accepts images from the memory bank of the subconscious, projecting them on to the solid backdrop of reality. Nothing that an alcoholic sees in the state of delirium tremens is new or real. At one time or another in his past life, all the figments of his hallucinations were witnessed in the physical sense, either in books, movies, or merely in the course of everyday observation. Consciously, he has forgotten all about that horror movie he saw when he was ten years old, but the creature in it – the fly with the head of a man – was so horrifying that it was traumatically impressed on his subconscious mind. Assisted by abject, but reasonable fear and anxiety during withdrawal, the alcoholic might experience an upsurge from the subconscious, and see the huge fly with a man's head seated on the edge of his bed. At times, so sensitized does the mind of the alcoholic become, that dreams and reality merge with continuity, so that he is unable to tell one state from the other . . .'

With his eyes tightly shut, he lay listening to the voice in his head. The appalling stench of the soaked mattress overcame his desire to rest upon it. Sitting up, he swung his legs off the bed and felt around for the can of water. There was something in his mouth; something that felt like a strip of unprocessed perlemoen or abalone. Moving the thing around, he discovered that it was his tongue. He found the can and had a good swallow of warm water; then, as he had done on numerous previous occasions, he placed his hands over his eyes — like a child playing peek-a-boo — and hoping that she had gone away, he peeped through his fingers. She was still there, looking much as she had looked in the hospital: tall, angular, hands thrust into the pockets of her white coat, an encouraging little smile on her long, pleasant, horse-like face. But now she was standing quite still and silent, as if frozen. Shutting his eyes again he felt in his pocket and found the box with its remaining cigarette. The matches were damp, but eventually he managed to light the crumpled tube. It tasted surprisingly good, and he sat smoking and staring at the floor, wondering how long he had slept. The room was darker now, so very likely the sun had moved down the sky. He found that he was not capable of protracted thought. Even though he experimented with a few ideas, they were snipped off, and curled away into nothingness.

'*. . . on very rare occasions, the alcoholic will experience a schizoid state of mind in which he will have visions that are projections of earlier and very real daydreams; possibly childhood or early post-puberty daydreams . . .*' He tapped his temples with the tips of his fingers, but the voice remained loud and clear in his head '*. . . even in so advanced a stage as early middle-age, quite suddenly, for no apparent reason, the alcoholic might come face to face with the man he aspired to be as a youth. These visions are brief, and seldom recalled . . .*'

He sat bolt upright, and the figment that was Doctor Milly Mayhew wavered, dimmed, and was gone from his mind, leaving the incredible statement: '*Face to face with the man he aspired to be as a youth*'. His body was possessed suddenly of an excruciating iciness in the heat of the room, as he recalled the man who had come through the old back gate ahead of Ben Gunn: the officer with the curiously familiar face — *his own face!* His face as it would have been, unravaged by years of alcoholism! Curling up on the filthy bed, he buried his face in his hands, and an ugly little whimpering sound escaped his lips.

After a while, his sobbing subsided, and he knew that the kewpie was in the room: he could hear the whirring of its tiny wings. 'Why don't you say a prayer?' piped the tiny voice in his head. 'Say after me:

God grant me the Serenity
to accept the things I cannot change.
Courage to change the things I can
and the Wisdom to know the difference.'

The awful goat-shed grew darker and quieter, and even the evening sounds of District Six beyond the tin walls seemed to recede.

He began to drift off into a strange void of shifting colours; a world in which time seemed to expand and contract and fold in on itself, and sounds and smells were heightened visual sensations. There were scenes of long-forgotten incidents and places, in which he was at once both the observer and the observed. He was attired in his white number six uniform, his impeccable cap tilted at just the right angle, and the gold-braid flashed on his epaulettes as he walked through the gates of Keppel Harbour. Despite the humid, oriental-scented evening air, there was a spring in his step. He was young and bronzed and as handsome as the very devil. Beyond the harbour gates, in the Empire Road, stood the chop-house of the Scarlet Moon. He entered in his usual breezy manner. The place was crowded, but he found a place at a zinc-topped table, at which sat a grubby bearded fellow with a tiny gold ear-ring in his left ear. The bum was shirtless, which was not unusual in such a place, for the Singapore waterfront abounded in curious characters of all nations. 'Maak 'n las vir a dop, ou Whitey,' said the 'bo, indicating his empty enamel mug.

Beaming upon the bum, for in him he recognised a kindred soul, he clapped his hands, and very soon a little old man wearing a white jacket with 'Fred's Chicken Grill' stitched in red above the pocket, served them with bottles of Tiger-Bone wine, and there was a saucer of tiny sesame cakes and salted water-melon seeds. With a delightful anticipation of meeting a beautiful girl he sat happily at ease, watching the mah-jongg players at their bewildering game. Dockyard workers were taking their evening meal and the fah-fee runner moved about the tavern, paying the winners of the morning 'pull' and taking the evening bets for the ancient numbers game of dreams and symbolism. Sew-sew girls in faded cotton trousers and baggy blouses came clacking along on their wooden leather-strapped clogs, their great round straw hats tied beneath their chins with coloured scarves. And each had a round basket of paraphernalia: needles and thread, buttons and scraps of patching, darning wool and clothes-pegs, poor simple things with which they earned a crust by darning and sewing and patching and washing and ironing the clothes of the hundreds of seamen in the dozens of ships lying in the great harbour of the Lion City. Weary now, after working all the long tropical day, and rowing their sampans from ship to ship, they sat at a long table, and he watched them sipping their green tea and taking their rice and fish with rapid chop-sticks. A loud slap slap slap at the mah-jongg table told of the fall of the East Wall, and the voices of the players rose in excitement, and the Tiger-Bone wine was pleasantly warm in his stomach.

A Chinese child of about six years came to stand at the table. She was an exquisite, doll-like little creature, dressed in a floral-print skirt and a snowy blouse, her little feet tucked into the patent-leather straps of her tiny clogs. She held a curious little eight-stringed harp, and began to play upon it a plinky-plinky little tune, which sounded like an oriental version of 'Show me the way to go home'. And all the while as she played, her eyes were fixed on the bearded character in the straw-basher and gold-striped tie. So inscrutable were her almond eyes, so serious was her expression, that he found that he was unable to move until the little tune was finished. And then he scratched in the pocket of his jeans for a coin of nickel, and the Tiger-Bone wine turned to ice in his stomach. '*Jeans?*' piped the tiny voice of the kewpie.

He sat clad only in his bright-blue skants, and in his hand was a little buff-coloured ticket, which he tucked into the pocket of the child's blouse. She took it out and began to read in a high, clear sing-song voice: 'SAR & H — EAST LONDON STATION BAGGAGE — 5c.'

A scream bubbled up in his throat, and it was the only sound in the great gloomy hall, furnished with foam-rubber couches and dark cabinets, richly glowing. In the walls were carved windows latticed with rice-paper, through which a moonshine light filtered from without, high-lighting the gilt edgings of the furniture and the crimson edges of the high beams. Upon the walls hung dozens of gold-framed pictures of a departed deity or general with an unsmiling face and unfeeling eyes. A maroon lacquered table with blackwood legs stood in the centre of the hall, and at it was seated a man wearing the blue uniform of the Merchant Navy. The four gold rings on his sleeves glinted in the unreal light. Set before the officer was an upturned goblet and a golden flagon sealed with a hideous scarlet devil's head. The man sat as still as an idol, his eyes fixed on the reflection in the golden flagon.

He tried to reach the captain, to explain why the reflection in the golden flagon appeared to be that of a dirty, scrounging, half-dressed bum, but as he drew closer to the table he was driven back by a ghastly miasma of food smells. Time and again he tried to cross the floor, waving his arms to attract attention, but all his efforts failed, and finally he turned sadly away. The little girl took his hand, and led him towards a massive, carved doorway, beyond which he could see bright sunlight, and the passing to and fro of a great many people, cars and trishaws. At the doorway the child released his hand, and he looked into her eyes, which were like tiny windows in her waxen face, through which he looked down the centuries into the Middle Kingdom with its exquisite art of the Mings. Then before his horrified eyes the child began to change: her eyes died and her hair grew lank and coarse about the ancient pitted face, and her body took on the lifeless humanoid form of a rag doll. 'Raindrops are falling on my bed,' the doll sang in a squeaky voice.

'*. . . as the alcoholic continues the ingestion of alcohol,*' said Doctor Milly Mayhew, '*so the secretion of toxic acetaldahyde increases. The toxin builds up in the spinal column and the brain becomes so saturated that its malfunctioning reaches a point of no return called Korsakoff psychosis. Spatial time and continuity collapse, and dreams and reality intermingle. Korsakoff psychosis is incurable, but not physically terminal. At this stage, if he is lucky the alcoholic dies; if not he will live out the remainder of his life with no more mentality than a cabbage . . .*'

He rushed through the great curved portal into the narrow sloping China-smelling street. Panic-stricken he hurried along the pavement, but no-one among the throng of people paid the least attention to him. One after another the papier-mâché buildings loomed up and sped away, and the vertical banners bearing Chinese characters stood out stiffly as though lashed by a great wind.

An ancient crone appeared suddenly before him: a materialisation, it seemed, of the nebulous stuff of departed time. The old woman thrust a thing in his face. It was thin and grey and scaly like the severed claw of some long-dead eagle — a hand! He peered into the shawl that covered her head and saw a wedge-shaped skull with a fine set of canines but no other teeth. '*Oulemmus Regionis Sextae!*' the skull screamed. 'Ek sal djou kry, witvark!' The familiar words followed him as he fled along the seemingly endless street. On and on he ran, and when it seemed that his lungs would burst, he hailed an old Ford Prefect taxi. Boon was at the wheel and beside him, on the front seat, was the corpse of a Sea Point skolly with a knife in its throat. Boon passed across a bottle of sweetwine, which tasted like carbide. He spewed a long liver-coloured jet over the side of the trishaw they had acquired, and Boon peddled furiously to escape a patrol-van bearing the tubular blue light of the South African Police, driven by a fox-faced gent in a dark suit. On and on they rushed through the teeming streets of the never-sleeping city beneath the eerily-green, flood-lit Cathay Building. Up South-bridge Road — banked on either side with green fibre suitcases — down Lavender Street, where the allnite whores sat on tiny stools around the allnite coffee-stalls. 'You want jig-jig, Charlie? Two dollar short time,' they called after him.

He felt splendidly handsome in his dove-grey cadet's uniform, with the flashing brass buttons and the orange-white-and-blue twisted cord at the lapels, his impeccable cap set at just the right angle.

Boon braked to a halt outside the gate of the Happy World, and there stood Manya, beautiful in a cheongsam of the purest yellow silk, with a showered pattern of the tiny scarlet-tipped buds of the bird's foot lotus, the high chaste collar embroidered with silver-thread dragons.

Arm-in-arm they moved down the fantastic midway of the carnival of the Happy World. Up and around they were swept in a car of the great spinning wheel; and then in a roller-coaster, screaming down the rails, yelling with soundless delight as the myriad fireworks exploded in a shower of multi-coloured stars. Time and again, he lost Manya in the crush of happy brown and yellow bodies; and each time he found her she was dressed in different exotic clothes: now a creation in jade-green, now lavender, now peach, and once, for a brief erotic moment she wore only a gorgeous lotus-flower in her shining black hair. In a languid embrace, they drifted through the Tunnel of Love, while gold and silver music cascaded down the walls of the intimately-lighted cavern of erotically twisting forms. He found her lovely face in his hands, and as they drew closer, he could smell the perfume of her parted lips — then, there was chaos in his head and the sound of a terrible grey wind. The grey wind moaned and died and Manya was gone, and he wandered through the sulphury, dripping cavern. 'Manya!' he cried in his anguish and loneliness, and from the dark corners of the cavern came a thousand dark echoes: 'Manya . . . Manya . . . Manya is gone forever!'

Forever he whirled backwards, growing ever smaller, engulfed in a silent sphere of shifting colours—like a soap-bubble floating in midday space. The sphere expanded and grew ever brighter, and he gazed into the endless bright distance; then two icy fingers gently closed his eyelids, for only the dead may look into eternity.

'Why . . . tee. Why . . . tee.'

A voice! A human voice at the end of a long blue tunnel — and a stench of appalling intensity!

6

i

He struggled in the depths of some hellish pit of filthy slime. The stench was nauseating, but after a while he ceased to struggle, for the sensation of choking to death was passing, and it seemed that he had returned from a strange and distant dream. For a moment he lay quite still, not daring to open his eyes, for he did not know who or where he was. Then he felt a cool hand on his brow.

'Whitey, are you awake?'

Instinctively he put his hand over his eyes and peeped through his fingers. The voice came from the dark silhouette of a woman standing beside the bed. She was holding a candle above her head, so that its gleam fell upon his body. The woman lowered the candle, and he saw that it was Manya, dressed in dark slacks and a high-neck sweater. As he struggled from the depths of sleep, he saw that the door of the room was ajar, and a pale shaft of moonlight struck across the filthy floor.

The girl bent closer and peered at him. 'You seem to have been having a terrible dream. You were twisting and turning and moaning as though you were in pain. Are you all right?'

Gradually, he adjusted to reality, while the shards of the dream melted and vanished like chip-ice in the sun. He felt thick and wooden, and his mouth was an awful maw of dried-out slime. Raising himself on his elbows, he inched back until he was resting against the bedhead. Then, aware of a mounting sense of shame and embarrassment, he looked at Manya. 'Yes, I think I'm all right. Hellish thirsty. Excuse me please.' He reached down for the can, and found that it was full, and the water quite cool. Someone — perhaps Eddie — must have come in while he was asleep. Rinsing his mouth, he drank a little of the sweet water; then he tried to gather and correlate the facts of the day and his existence in it. His head felt brittle, but bit by bit he pieced the day together. It seemed to have been a very short day, indeed. He looked at the girl, searching her shadowy face for any signs of disapproval or disgust, but there was none. 'If I remember correctly, you went to work this morning. Did you have a good day, Manya?'

'Oh, so you do remember me,' she smiled. Dripping some wax on to a narrow shelf at the side of the bed, she settled the candle, then seated herself gingerly on the edge of the bed. 'Phew! This place stinks. Did you sleep all the time?'

'What time is it?'

'It's after eight o'clock.' Lighting two cigarettes, she passed one across. 'I had the usual sort of day. Rushed. We're very busy at this time of the year.' She looked him over carefully, her eyes scanning his chest and arms. 'You didn't get into trouble today?'

'Not really. I had a bit of a run-in with the cops. Ou Lem wanted to beat me up, but Mommy stopped him. Do you mean that sort of trouble?'

'I wanted to warn you to be careful — before I left this morning. Ou Lem had been boasting about how he was going to beat you up . . .'

'Why didn't you warn me?'

'I'm sorry, Whitey. But that ou Lem is such a mad thing. I thought that it was perhaps just empty boasting, and I didn't think that you would stay so long. Besides, you might have been annoyed: it is not a woman's job to tell a man to be careful of another. You . . . well . . . you might have thought that I was trying to pull my petticoat over your head.'

It was a curious expression, and he smiled to himself, in spite of the rising nausea and the cramps creeping up his legs. 'Well, no harm done, Manya. I did intend to move off this morning, but one thing led to another and before I knew what was happening, I was drunk again. Then Mommy fed me, and Eddie locked me in here.' He looked at Manya, feeling his affection for her growing. 'I really can't understand why you people bother with me at all. I must buzz off now. I feel that I have over-stayed my welcome.' He stood up too quickly, and his head smashed against a beam, sending him reeling back in agony. He lay gasping on the bed, while Manya stood up and bent over him.

'Whitey! What is it; what happened?'

The white-hot agony slowly subsided, and he sat up slowly. 'My head,' he said faintly. 'I hit it on that . . . '

'You didn't hit it on anything, Whitey! There is nothing up there but the beams: four feet above your head, when you're standing.' She was staring at him, her eyes wide with concern. 'Whitey . . . you're . . . not well, I think. Let me get a taxi and take you up to Groote Schuur.'

He found the cigarette that had fallen from his fingers, then he took her hand as she sat beside him. 'Groote Schuur Hospital, Manya? You would be wasting your time and I would be wasting theirs. I have been through it all before. They would give me a wallop of paraldehyde to knock me out and chase away the horries, and in forty-eight hours' time, when I wake up, they'll find my mind and tighten the screws; they'll feed me and give me lots of TLC . . .'

'What's TLC, Whitey?' There was a hint of awe in her whispered question as she gazed at him with big, child-like eyes.

'Tender loving care, Manya. And when I have recovered physically, they'll explain exactly what ails me, using big words and high-sounding phrases. They'll tell me exactly how I will end up if I take another drink. And then when I'm radiant with physical health, they'll turn me out on the street, and within a week I'll be drunk again, because all their tools, their big words and knowledge, have not been able to reach deep down to the fundamental faults which lie buried and festering in the depths of the psychological make-up of people such as me. I am one of the oddballs that medical science seems unable to reach. But God bless them for the way they try.' His head was splitting, but he smiled at Manya, who seemed to be in a minor trance. Her lips were parted, and her eyes were fixed on something in the gloom behind him. After a long moment of silence, she looked at him again.

'Oh, Whitey, I wish I could understand. All I know is that when people drink too much they get sick . . . I mean sick at the stomach. What are these faults you speak about, Whitey?'

'Perhaps a compound of a lot of things, Manya. Perhaps it even goes back beyond my mother's womb.'

She withdrew her hand, and seemed to shrink away from him. 'I wish I could understand,' she said again.

'Don't be afraid of me, Manya,' he said quickly. 'Perhaps I've made it sound sort of spooky, but it isn't really.'

'Oh, I'm not afraid. I was just thinking how awful it must be for you. Like a . . . like a disease, né?' She nodded her head eagerly, like a child aware that it has given the correct answer to a riddle.

'Yes, something like that. But don't you worry about me. I've been like this before; it'll wear off.' *Or you'll croak it this time,* he added to himself. 'Perhaps you'll be good enough to ask Willy if he has an old shirt for me? I have been meaning to ask him all day, but somehow I never was able to get to the point. Then perhaps the boys will give me a walk down to Darling Street?'

Manya fiddled with her cigarette box and matches. Obviously nervous about something, she stood up and looked out of the door, then she came back to the bed and stood looking down at him. 'The boys are not at home. They've gone to bioscope. Whitey, you can't go anywhere in your state. Even with the boys, you wouldn't get very far. This is District Six, and it is Saturday night. The police are prowling around and there are gangs. Even if you reached town, what would you do in your state; where would you go? Mommy says you belong in East London.'

'What about Boon; perhaps he'll . . . ?'

'*Boon!* You can't trust Boon. You can never trust any skolly, Whitey. In any case, if the police haven't got him he'll be so *gerook* by this time that he probably won't even recognise you.' Patently agitated now, she lit another cigarette for him, and stamped out the mangled thing he had been trying to smoke, then she said slowly, 'You're not even safe in the yard, Whitey.

There are some who come here who don't like white people — they don't like anyone other than their own kind. Mommy has a certain control over ou Lem and Boon: they need her and she needs them for protection against other gangs. Boon's gang is called the Gympie Street Crew, and this is their area. But if they decide to beat a man up, Mommy won't be able to stop them. In that lane out there, or in the street, they might kill you.' Manya hastily lit another cigarette for herself. 'When they are full of dagga and spirits, they don't care about anything. Their whole *thing* is violence. Prison doesn't frighten them; they laugh at prison, and even execution. They're awful, and I hate them. They give us *such* a bad name. They do terrible things, and then the newspapers print stories about them, and people in the other parts of the country think that we're all skollies and loafers. I don't mean that everybody thinks this way, but a lot of people do — even in Cape Town! It makes me sick, Whitey. Most of us are just ordinary people, living ordinary, everyday lives.'

Quite angry now, Manya stood up and snuffed the candle. 'Ugh, how this room stinks!' she hissed. 'It stinks of skollies!' She took his hand again. 'Come, Whitey, Mommy wants to see you.'

Beyond the tin walls, the violent undertones of the voice of District Six seemed to grow in volume. In his mind's eye, he saw the tall dark shadows moving stealthily along the narrow, twisting streets and lanes. He saw the littered, broken pavements, the tiny, cobbled squares, lost to history for half a century or more. And the old houses, and the clusters of ancient buildings, grossly overcrowded with humans, pets and rats: fire-traps and incubators for disease: a festering sore that would remain forever on the souls of the grasping, neglectful landlords, sitting counting coins in fine suburban homes.

The sadness in the dying soul of District Six seemed to permeate his own being, bringing with it a hopelessness and the first edging-in of fear. He knew that if he lay there much longer, he would not be able to get off the bed. The cramps had reached his knees, and his feet were like blocks of ice. It occurred to him that if there was any reason why he should get up and go anywhere at all, he was unable to see it. Perhaps Mommy would have 'trouble with the authorities', but they would not be *his* troubles. He looked up at the girl silhouetted against the moonlit doorway, and the love that he felt was an amalgam of gratitude and sympathy. And in the face of her courage, he felt small and humble. 'Manya,' he said softly. 'I don't want you or Mommy to go to any more trouble on my account. If you'll do just one last little thing for me — if you'll just get me a bottle of soetes, and then lock me in here. When it is light, someone can let me out, and I'll just fade down the lane and . . .'

'No! Mommy has something to say to you, and you need to eat and clean yourself up.' She moved to the door and looked out. 'Come on, Whitey.'

He could see no point in further argument, and once free of the awful room he felt a little better. The yard of La Residence Stilhuis was deserted, bathed in spectral moonlight. 'It's quiet,' he said, as he hobbled across towards the house, 'Business must be bad.'

'The back gate is always bolted at night. Mommy will allow no-one in the yard, and only special customers in the house. The gate used to be left open, but a few years ago there was a terrible gang-fight in here. In the morning the police found seven corpses in the lane: three men and four dogs. Ever since then the gate has been kept bolted. Now she smokkles from the window of a room at the side of the house. It is only a gap between the buildings, but a man can get up there to the window.'

'The old girl has certainly got it made. Who is in the house now?'

'Well, old Ben is in the voorkamer, giving orders and firing cannons at the Japanese ships. That old vark's mad, but he's harmless. And then there is only Mommy and brother Leo. He's from the New Gospel Hope Tabernacle in Hannover Park, where Mommy goes.'

He hung behind Manya as they entered the kitchen. Mommy Stilhuis was seated at the kitchen table, and sitting opposite her, his hands folded reverentially in his lap, was a sharp-faced, neatly dressed Coloured man of early middle-age. He had all the hall-marks, the slack wet lips, the shifty eyes and the ingratiating smile of certain sectarian lay-preachers who use the cross and the gullibility of simple people for their own devious ends. The roving hot eyes picked up and followed Manya as she moved across the kitchen to stand at Mommy's side. Then, like insects, the eyes crawled slowly up the girl's body, stopping briefly here and there, then moving on again, to roll up her red sweater and have a good feel of her naked breasts; and then down again, under the waist-band of her slacks, to caress the silky mound between her thighs. Manya moved behind Mommy's chair, and Brother Leo produced a snowy handkerchief to dab his glistening brow.

Well to the leeward of the table — for there was a slight draft from the direction of the doorway — he stood there, dejected and evil-smelling, for almost a minute, before Mommy looked at him, and when she did look, it was as if she had never seen him before. There was a curl to her lips and her eyes were inscrutable. Manya fiddled with the cuffs of her sweater; her manner was altogether that of a child who has found a stray kitten and is awaiting the verdict of its fate: doom or deliverance. She flashed him a brief encouraging smile, then Brother Leo turned to give him his full attention — and he was no longer smiling.

'For the glutton and the drunkard shall come to poverty,' Brother Leo intoned solemnly. 'Look thou not upon the wine when it is red, for at last it biteth like a serpent, and stingeth like an adder.'

'Amen!' Mommy responded with righteous vehemence. *'Holy Jesus,* never in my life have I seen a filthier-looking piece of rubbish! Gertie, give him a towel and let him have a bath. He's stinking up the whole house!'

Perhaps Mommy's tough attitude and disparaging remarks were intended to reduce him to a state of complete self-revulsion — a despicable standpoint from which to take cognizance of himself. It was an old trick of the uninitiated do-gooders. He felt too weak and sick now to be angry; but he wanted to protest, to make it known that the bed was filthy and that he had been sweating for hours in the furnace of a room. But even as he opened his mouth to speak, Mommy turned away in disgust, and began to discuss with Brother Leo the costs of the addition to the Tabernacle.

He looked helplessly at Manya, who indicated with her head that he should follow her. She waited for him in the middle of the short passage. 'This is the bathroom,' she said, pointing to a closed door. 'You wait here while I get you a towel and soap.' She smiled. 'And I have something else for you.'

'I hope it's a bottle of soetes,' he moaned, half to himself.

'What?'

'Nothing Tell me, Manya, what happened to the old one?'

Manya looked at him blankly. 'What do you mean, Whitey? What old one?'

'The *Old* Gospel Hope Tabernacle — I expect it went out of business because all the choir-girls got mysteriously pregnant.'

'I still don't . . .' Manya's face was a picture, lovely and puzzled '. . . Oh you mean *him?* He' creepy. He always rubs against me.' She giggled. 'Now you wait right here. Don't go into the voorkamer; that old vark will get you drinking again.' She went off across the voorkamer and disappeared into the front passage.

Disturbed now by consciousness and physical movement, the slumbering demons stirred. He wanted desperately to sit down somewhere. His knees and ankles were aching, and his feet were sore and tender. He felt very old and tired, and he was conscious of an increasing sensation of unreality. Perhaps this place was an illusion? Perhaps this was where he came when the blackness of amnesia beset him? Perhaps he would soon return to reality in some totally different place; a peaceful park or a sunny, deserted beach?

'On the beam a submarine; the biggest bastard I've ever seen! All guns load with H.P. sauce. Ha! Ha! Ha!'

The shocking barking reverberating voice assaulted his ears from the direction of the voorkamer; then Mommy came moving rapidly down the passage. She swept past him, almost smearing him along the wall. At the end of the passage, she stopped and stood with her hands on her massive hips. 'Hey, you, Ben! Keep quiet! This is not a bloody warship. Any more of that, and I'll throw you out into the back room — without your wine!'

There was no answer from the voorkamer — no sound. Then Mommy returned down the passage, and he flattened himself against the bathroom door, in the meagre recess, as the giantess thundered past, to return to the kitchen table. When the old woman had settled herself, he crept towards the voorkamer, poked his head around the door-jamb and looked straight into two mad black eyes.

For a long moment, they stared at each other in disbelief, like two castaways coming face-to-face on an island; the one not daring to believe that the other filthy, bearded, tangled thing was real. Then a cunning gleam appeared in Ben Gunn's eyes, and he beckoned with a long finger, indicating the half-full can on the table, and making drinking motions with the other hand. Then, pouring a full glass of wine, he slid it across the table, in a very tempting manner. At that moment, Manya reappeared.

He drew back quickly, salivating, and in his frustration he began to tremble and shake. Never before had the rattles beset him so quickly. The demons were wide awake! Staggering under the onslaught of the phantom with the ice-pick, he fell back against the door, digging his nails into the wood. Manya came towards him. She was smiling as she held out the bundle of things. 'Here's a towel and soap,' she said. 'And a shirt and a pair of slip-slops. They're not new, but the shirt is freshly ironed. Why are you hanging your head like that; why don't you look at me?'

With a great effort, he managed to lift his exploding head. 'Manya,' he said. 'Please believe me . . . I . . .I don't feel like a bath. I feel . . . well . . . awful. I just want to go back to that room and lie down. Won't you just lock me in that room?'

'No, Bokkie, you'll feel so much better after a bath. You're filthy, and it'll freshen you up. Then perhaps Mommy will give you just a tiny glass of wine. Take these things, Whitey.' She bundled the towel and clothing into his arms, and opening the door she pushed him into the bathroom. 'There, have a nice bath and I'll see to some food for you.'

ii

The door closed behind him, and he slid down and sat on the floor. 'Ooooh, Christ,' he moaned aloud. 'Have a nice bath. Coming up, one wine-marinaded, cleaned and dressed long-pig for the midnight feast of the Gympie Street Crew. Ooooh Lord!'

For a couple of minutes he sat on the floor, staring at the old-fashioned toilet with the split seat. Mentally and physically he was at the lowest ebb that he could remember. 'Must be the famous rock-bottom', he muttered. The nausea was increasing and there was the occasional sharp jab in the pit of his stomach, and the sinister suggestion of bile secreting from the liver —

in the wrong direction; and his head felt conical rather than domed. At length, whilst trying to still the rattles, in a disconsolate sort of way he examined the things which Manya had given him, and he all but blubbed because of her kindness. The rubber slip-slops were practically new, and so was the shirt — a violently-hued thing with spangles and stars and crazy arabesques: a madman's dream of the Spiral Nebula.

After a while, with his consciousness receding and returning like a badly tuned radio station, he found that the possession of the cheap gear gave him quite an uplift: he was moving in the right direction. All that he had to do, really, was to have the goddamn bath, get dressed, have a glass of wine. And then? Well . . . ask Mommy to get him a taxi, and fade. He nodded his head in agreement. It was as easy as that — until he tried to get up and implement his plan. But he was stiff, frozen. His brain had lost contact with his legs. Try as he might, he was unable to move his legs; they might very well have belonged to someone else. In a panic now, he experimented with his toes — nothing, no movement; they were curled back stiffly, the big one of his right foot sticking up through a hole in his sock, like a piece of cold marble. He tried relaxing completely, and then after another minute, he had another go at it. Did the toe move, or was it an illusion? It was hard to tell. He slumped back against the door, and it was at that moment that he saw the spider.

It came out from under the old bath-tub, a grey-green spider, moving rapidly. He watched it in horror. A foot away from the tub it altered direction, and the light caught its bright ruby eyes. It came on towards him, and he found that he was standing up against the door, gibbering out of fear. The spider stopped and looked up at him, as if sizing him up. Dropping his things, he leaped into a corner and put his hands over his eyes and peeped through the fingers. The spider was still there; but as he watched, the creature skirted his towel and went out under the door. Was it real? He couldn't be sure. Perhaps it had gone away to round up its friends? Soon a million of them would come streaming back under the door. Tip-toeing to the laundry-basket, he found a soiled towel and arranged it along the bottom of the door; then feeling a little more secure, he dumped his things on a chair and looked around the bathroom.

It was about a hundred years old, light-grey in colour, with a high pressed-steel ceiling in the process of parting company with the walls. The half-inch gap was black and feathery with filth. The old tub stood on four claw-like feet, and there was an electric cylinder and a wash-hand basin of obviously recent installation. The tub proved to be fairly clean, but there was a black tear-shaped pattern down the centre — the narrow end at the plug-hole — where the enamel had been worn away by generations of bare, abrasive bottoms.

There was plenty of hot water, but it sprayed rather than flowed from a tap marked 'cold'. He adjusted the taps, and while the bath was running up, he had a look at his face in the mirror — which was either a bad one, or his face had grown longer and thinner since last he had seen it. His hair and beard were tangled, his eyes wild-looking and bloodshot. He looked terrible: somewhat like a self-portrait of Van Gogh at his worst! Turning away, he felt that one day he would look in a mirror and see nothing at all. To divert his senses away from the mounting compulsion, he did all sorts of trivial things: he had another look at his new gear, felt in his pockets for the cigarette he knew very well was not there. He thought about birds and mountains and rivers; and then he hung his head over the wash-basin and gave his mouth a good burst of cold water, allowing far too much of it into his stomach. The exploding acid shot up his throat and into the basin, bringing with it a grey, slimy liquid. After cleaning the basin, he stood shivering and rattling as he dropped his jeans and skants. The sight of his bowed legs, covered with gingery hair, increased the sourness at his stomach, and he got hurriedly into the bath — and was immediately inspired! '*Eureka!*' he cried gladly. 'I have it! Ben Gunn!'

Had not the old man offered him a drink? Was he a child to be told to do this or that? No! He would go and fetch a drink. Without bothering to dry himself, he rattled back into his jeans and found that he was making glad little whimpering sounds, like a welcoming puppy. He dried his face and almost ripped the door from its hinges, and there stood Manya, an ugly expression of surprise and fear on her face. Her hand and arm were raised in an attitude of knocking, and hanging over his head, like the Sword of Damocles, was a brand-new tooth-brush, still in its plastic wrapper. With a little cry, the girl stepped back. 'Whitey! What . . . you look terrible!'

'It's my mouth! I can't stand my mouth . . . I er . . . was going to look for a *tooth-brush!*'

'Well, isn't it a funny thing, Manya said, with feigned flippancy. 'A sort of coincidence.' She was calmer now, but he felt the trembling of her hand as she handed him the *poxy pink goddamn son-of-a-bitch plastic tooth-brush!* She backed down the passage. 'Don't be long. Your coffee and sandwiches will soon be ready. My room is the first one on the left in the front passage.'

He closed the door, this time remembering to slide the latch. Shot through with panic and fearful anxiety, he vowed that he would get into the bath and sleep, and that only the fire-brigade from Roeland Street would get him out. 'Oh, Lord,' he said to the face in the mirror, 'What a helpless hapless creature is a suffering drunk. Surely there must be at least one of the Heavenly Company who is willing to take up our cause as a patron?' Shivering and sweating, he shed his jeans and climbed painfully into the bath.

The taps were still open, and the water was very high in the tall old tub. Shutting them off, he turned on his side, drawing his knees up to his chest and sliding down until he was completely submerged. For some fifteen seconds, he lay in the foetal position in the cast-iron womb, and he began to die. He saw a tiny, old-world cobbled square, cold and mist-shrouded, and a cat that crouched on the cobbles: a sway-backed scruffy alley-cat with one baleful eye and a mangled ear. The creature was lapping with good appetite at a trickle of blood which wound like a rivulet through the canyons of the cobbles. In a very short time the cat reached the source of the rivulet and continued its meal with relish and impunity, licking at the blood-spattered face of the man who lay supine and helpless in his agony. In horrible fascination, he gazed at the familiar bearded face beneath the wild thatch of sandy hair, and at the gold ear-ring in the man's left ear.

His scream bubbled to the surface of the water, and spluttering and puking a little out of fear and revulsion, he strove to drive the picture from his mind. After some seconds of banging his head against the side of the tub, he found a little respite; then there was an urgent call from his bowels. Struggling breathlessly out of the tub, he sat on the toilet, clawing pitilessly at the sides of his head. Presently physical relief came in the form of a heavy gaseous effluvium rising from the pan. He felt less bloated and at least a kilogram lighter. It occurred to him that Mommy's spicy brown stew certainly had great purgative powers. The nausea was passing, and only the shivering and rattling remained, for they were of the mind, and only alcohol would dispel them.

Completing his stool, he got back into the bath and noticed that, preoccupied with the onset of the horries and then Manya's startling appearance at the door, he had omitted to remove his filthy black socks. He took them off and examined his long-suffering feet, which he had not seen for some time. They were tender and raw, but there were no serious abrasions or cuts. Getting out of the bath for the third time, he dumped his socks in the trash-can. On the wall beside the mirror was a cabinet of somewhat rustic design. It had very likely started life as a fruit-box, but now, fitted with a door, it contained the usual assortment of toilet requisites of a family. He scratched around in it, looking for a pair of scissors, and there, at the back of the cabinet, in all its lovely purple glory was a practically full bottle of vlam! For a long moment he stood there, looking at it, praying that it was not a figment. Then sweating, and with shaking hand, he reached slowly into the cabinet and took the bottle out. He shook it. It was real! A great sense of elation swept through him, carrying off the shakes, the rattles and the gloomy fears, for in his hand was the finest, short-order disperser of the horries that a suffering drunk could wish to find.

In a happy little mood now, he rinsed a tooth-glass and poured an inch of meths into it, topping it up with water until it was a lovely sky-blue colour and the glass grew warm from the chemical reaction set up by the poison and the water; then he knocked it back, hovering over the toilet, for the first shot of vlam on an empty stomach is always unpredictable. This one, however, stayed down. There was the ghastly chemical taste in his mouth, and he was conscious of the spirit gouging its way through the tissues of his digestive tract, into his stomach, killing or maiming umpteen millions of cells en route. Then there was only the foul taste in his mouth, and the warm welcome glow spreading throughout his system.

He found a pair of manicure scissors in an old Elastoplast tin in the cabinet. Pouring himself another hooker of vlam, he got back into the tub, and began a painful operation on his feet. 'Oh, if only there were gold under them long black toe-nails,' he mused.

The second hooker of vlam settled in very well indeed. Other than the sinister burning in the pit of his stomach and the occasional flicker of his eyes, caused by the denatured spirit attacking his optic nerve, the two glasses of meths seemed to have had no detrimental effect on his general health — the little that was left of it. Whistling while he worked, presently he began to feel a little peckish, and his spirits rose another notch when he thought about the food that Manya was preparing. The very idea of eating it in her room and in her company was also uplifting. He bent to his task with renewed effort. He felt, however, that what he really needed for the nails of his big toes was a pair of mechanic's side-cutters. He had bent the scissors a bit, but most of the horn-like growth had joined the rest of the mire at the bottom of the tub. At length, he gave his feet a gentle scrub with the brush he found in the rusty little basket at the side of the bath. His feet refurbished, he lathered himself liberally with Manya's soap, and the water darkened with the filth that came out of his hair.

The bathroom door creaked under pressure from the passage side, and a voice called, 'Hurry up! Other people want to use the bathroom!'

It sounded like Brother Leo, and he told the preacher firmly to go and get stuffed! Then stepping out of the tub, he stood steaming on the mat. After drying himself he stood still, absolutely still and relaxed. They were still there, the rattles and the shakes were still there beneath the surface, temporarily subdued by the action of the meths on his nervous system. He knew that for a couple of hours he would look and feel reasonably normal. He had another shot of vlam for good measure, then gave his mouth a good scouring with the toothbrush, for a vlam-drinker exudes the distinct odour of a veteran primus stove.

As he began to dress, a mood of gloom descended upon him, and he was torn between the desire to head for Sea Point while he was able and to see Manya again. '*Take the bottle of meths,*' the dark voice said. He stopped combing his hair and looked at himself in the mirror. '*Put the bottle and the glass in your shirt and cut a line for Sea Point. It will be nice there under the Prom, quietly nibbling away at the bottle.*' Looking at the face in the mirror, he saw the beads of sweat beginning to form on the brow. The cheeks were gaunt, the eyes hollow. *'These people have been good to you,'* piped the tiny voice of the kewpie. He felt the tension of indecision building up within him, then a sort of rage shuddered through him as the dark voice said, *'These stupid people won't even miss you.'* 'You ungrateful bum!' he screamed at the face in the mirror.

PART TWO

Kismet

7

i

The girl who opened the door was a complete stranger. 'Well, a new man,' she said with a dazzling smile. She wore a pink padded house-gown, and her eyes twinkled behind a pair of shapely gold-rimmed spectacles. Her hair was done in braids, tied at the ends with little pink bows, and hung down over her breasts like hanks of black silk. Her face was scrubbed and shining, and she looked about sixteen years old. It was only when she canted her head and he noticed the dimple, that he realised that the girl was Manya.

She held a bright-jacketed novel in one hand, a finger tucked between the pages to keep her place, while the other hand fluttered chastely about the collar of the gown. 'You look quite strange, Whitey,' she continued. 'Now didn't I tell you that a nice hot bath would make a difference? Would you like to come in; I have sandwiches and coffee for you?'

'If I'm not intruding,' he said awkwardly, leaning back a little so as to keep her out of the range of his breath, which he was sure held the sharp smell of meths. 'You've had a long day and you're ready for bed. I could quite easily have the food in the kitchen.'

Manya grinned at him. 'Wouldn't you like to eat in Boon's room? A little while ago you were begging to get back there.'

'That's a cruel thing to say. I was feeling very sick.'

Manya chuckled and stood aside. 'Come in, Whitey. It is only nine o'clock and I can sleep all day tomorrow.'

She closed the door and snapped the latch. 'That's only to keep the prowlers out,' she said with the hint of a smile. 'You can sit over there on the dressing-stool.' She poured two cups of coffee from a jug; then with one of them in her hand she curled up on the big divan covered with a maroon counterpane. 'The sandwiches are all for you. Please eat them up.' Removing her glasses, she leaned back against a pile of pillows and sipped her coffee, watching him over the rim of the cup.

Settling himself on the stool at the dressing table, he chose a sandwich, feeling just about as false and out of place as a man could feel in such a feminine room and under such circumstances. 'Do you read a lot?' he asked, rather lamely, indicating the bookcase with its neat rows of bright-spined books.

'Yes I do. There is no entertainment in District Six — and not much more in town. I don't go out very much. I find plenty to do around the house, with Binty and Cookie to look after.'

He bit into the sandwich of fresh whole-wheat bread, lettuce and cheese, and the very minty smell of it brought home to him how starved his body was for fresh nutritious food. Chewing away, he looked around the room. Binty was in his cot. The little boy was fast asleep, his bottom stuck up in the air. 'You have a pleasant room, Manya. What do you do down at the factory in Salt River?' He was beginning to feel more relaxed, for the room held no evidence at all of male occupation.

'I work in the Despatch Department. We have a very big factory and we get orders from all over the country. I . . . we see to it that the orders go out on time . . . '

'I bet you're in charge down there,' he said, watching the deep rose colour creeping into her face.

'Well . . . yes . . . but only of the girls. You see, Whitey, I've been at the factory since I was fourteen years old. I started as a machinist's helper.'

He listened with growing admiration as Manya recounted how, by her own efforts and in her own time, she strove to improve her position, taking evening lessons and buying books on commercial subjects. 'Maybe you think I'm boasting, Whitey, but it's true. When I got my commercial JC they took me out of the factory and put me in the Despatch Department. And now I'm in charge of six girls — and one of them has a matric certificate!'

'I don't think you're boasting. I'm very proud of you, especially since Achmet Smit told me about your passion for education and how well you took care of the children. I bet Cookie is the only child of her age in District Six who can read.'

Manya's flush deepened, and in her soft, obviously carefully cultivated accent, she began to tell him a little of her childhood. 'My ou has never been a drunkard or a loafer, Whitey. He battled to buy me books and things so that I could go to school, but couldn't see why I wanted to carry on after I' could read and do sums. The older people are so ignorant about important things. But I suppose it's because of the way they had to live in their time; from hand to mouth, when every penny that anyone in the family earned meant more food. My ou found it difficult to keep a fourteen-year-old girl in food and clothing. I was badly dressed and nearly always hungry, but I stayed in school until I had passed standard six. Then I was on my own, and I made a promise to myself that if ever I had children their education would come before anything I might need.'

He found that he was unable to meet her eye, and he looked across to where the little child lay sleeping in his cot, and he wondered again about Binty, with his light complexion and curious grey eyes. Turning to the dressing table, he pushed the empty plate aside and refilled his coffee cup.

His eyes fell on a photograph in a small gilt frame. Without really meaning to pry he looked at it closely. It was a bust photograph in colour of a blonde young man dressed in the round-rig of the Royal Navy. The young sailor with smiling Anglo-Saxon face appeared, like Manya, to be in his mid-twenties, and like Binty he had curious wood-smoke grey eyes.

His question was answered, but on its heels followed other questions. Was the young Englishman aware of the responsibility that had been created in the heat of desire? Was the young man aware of the awesome implications? Even at its face value it was a sad, perhaps even a tragic thing, for the future was so uncertain. Turning away from the dressing-table, involuntarily his eyes strayed back to the cot where Binty lay asleep, utterly innocent and unsuspecting.

'That's Binty's father,' Manya said quietly, as she came up to replace her coffee-cup.

'He's a good-looking lad. When do you expect him back?'

For a long moment she was silent, gazing at the photograph as if in deep thought, then she said: 'They never come back, Whitey. We exchanged letters for a while, but I haven't heard from him for more than a year. His ship has left these waters, and by this time he would have finished his National Service. I will never see him again; I know this and I feel nothing.' She smiled. 'But I have Binty.'

'Does he know about the child?'

'No, and it would be wrong of me to tell him. He was sweet and kind, but I didn't know him long enough to really find out about his character. What happened between us was just a thing that happened. He didn't like South Africa very much and I would never live anywhere else. I love Cape Town and I love my people. Binty is my whole life and he will have everything that I am able to give him. Soon, we will be leaving District Six: Mommy has bought a house out at Athlone. Binty and me will be going along with the boys and Cookie. And I'll be glad. I'm sick and tired of all this noise and filth. Out there we'll be able to start to reshape our lives. Things are improving all the time for the Coloured people, and who knows perhaps by the time Binty is grown, all the ugliness will have passed away.' She turned suddenly and smiled down at him. 'You enjoyed your food, né?'

Startled out of the reverie induced by Manya's words, he looked up at the girl. 'Oh . . . yes . . . the food was fine. Thank you. And Manya, I must say that I admire your courage and faith.'

'What else must a mother do, ou Whitey?' She lit two cigarettes and passed one across. 'There. Since you have been so good and eaten your food, I'll see if Mommy has a glass of wine for you.' Flashing him another bright smile, she went out of the room.

He sat smoking, his mind beset with unhappy thoughts about the future of the little boy sleeping in the cot. On the credit side, Binty had health, beauty and the strength of character of his mother, but in the debit column? However, many other children from District Six had made it; just as from every ghetto in the world had come great human beings, to add to the sum total of man's knowledge in all fields of endeavour and activity. But it was going to be a tough uphill grind for little Binty, and for Cookie, who was 'nobody's child'.

He sat for some minutes feeling sad and lonely, not daring to look into his own future, for it always produced a suicidal wave of hopelessness. Fortunately he was soon distracted by the sounds of a number of people walking down the passage. He could distinguish several male voices, and then the giggles of girls. The sounds faded, and in a few minutes Manya came back. She latched the door with a loud snap.

'Mommy says that this all you're getting,' she said lightly, placing a glass of sweetwine at his elbow. 'And she says that now that you're nice and clean you can sleep on one of the couches in the voorkamer.' She grinned, and it was the silly curved enigmatic grin of a cartoon cat. 'Now won't that be nice?'

'I'm sure that it will be a vast improvement on Boon's shack,' he said, wondering about the funny smile. 'You know I really can't understand why you and Mommy are doing all this for me? I mean, there must be dozens of bums like me who come in here for booze?'

'You're not a bum, Whitey. Mommy says that you are a seaman, but you don't talk like any seaman that I've ever known. You talk . . . well . . . like an educated person. But it doesn't matter what you are,' she added hastily. 'We sort of like you. Mommy has a nose for people. If she didn't like you she would have kicked you off her stoep this morning. And I mean *kicked*. There is a soft heart in her big tough body, but she is a terrible woman if you make her cross.'

'And you, Manya; do you have a nose for people?'

Manya returned to the bed and seated herself, tucking the gown about her legs. 'Perhaps. I like you because you're different. It is so nice to talk to someone who speaks good English; someone who doesn't think that I'm mad because I buy books without pictures in them.' Suddenly changing the subject, she said, 'Some funny people have just come in.'

'I heard them in the passage. Customers?'

'Yes. Three gentoos, whores, and three English seamen: a big fair one and two black ones.' Her eyes widened. 'And Whitey, a funny-looking white girl. She looks like one of those Jesus-people. You know — perhaps you don't — they hang around Greenmarket Square, and give out papers about religion. They also have a sort of market in Loop Street.'

Don't the people who come in here keep you awake with their noise?'

'They don't really make a noise; Mommy doesn't allow it. In any case I wouldn't open that door, even if they were killing each other out there. Anyway that's why she keeps Boon and ou Lem and a few of the Gympie Street Crew in the yard.'

'Ah yes, the Gympie Street Crew,' he said evenly, drinking the small glass of wine, which tasted like water compared to the meths.

Manya was studying him carefully, a smile on her lips. 'I seem to have been doing all the talking,' she said. 'All I know about you is that you're a seaman from East London who drinks too much. But I'm sure that you haven't always been that way?'

What could he tell her? He felt no more like talking about his shabby past than flying to the moon; in fact he didn't feel like talking at all. The meths, the sandwiches and the wine had begun a three-pronged attack on his temporary state of well-being. Considering a counter attack, a part of his mind had for the past few minutes been occupied with the automatic thinking process of the drunk: *when, where and how could the next drink be procured?* There was the vlam in the bathroom of course, but he knew very well what a few more shots of that would do to him, and he wanted to be as fresh as possible when he hit the drag in the morning. On the other hand if he went to bed in his present delicate conditon, he was sure that he would not sleep. However weary his body was, his mind would churn away without respite, producing all sorts of ugly and frightening pictures. But perhaps a couple of glasses of jupe would cloud his senses enough to send him off to sleep. He wondered how much wine old Ben had left in his can.

'Well, Whitey?' Manya canted her head and gave him her cartoon cat smile. 'You look a little faraway. I suppose you have been listening to me, even though it must have been very dull?'

'Not at all dull,' he said jerking a little as he reached out to drag his mind back. 'And I've been listening very carefully. I think that you have great courage and moral fibre.'

'What's that; moral fibre?'

'Well . . . strength of character; something I seem to have lost; or perhaps never had, to any great degree. But don't bother yourself, your sweet self, may I add. I am beyond redemption. However, I still have enough moral fibre left to blame myself, and not the world and his wife, for giving me a raw deal. Now, to substantiate my miserable position in society, I have to view it through rose-coloured glasses for it to have any meaning, both for myself and the world at large. For my part, I see myself as a successful failure.' He chuckled at the expression on Manya's face as her eyes widened and narrowed in her effort to follow all this booze-induced nonsense.

'What on earth is a successful failure?' she asked.

'Well, let's say that if I had been a steady nine-to-fiver all my life, by this time I would have an excellent job — possibly my own business — my wife and a home and very likely a couple of rebellious kids who smoke pot for relaxation. I would in fact, be Joe Dokes, a stalwart of society, a pillar of Suburbia with its shrunken intellectual horizon, its false morality and phoney propriety. Having lied and connived my way successfully through the commercial week, I would spend lazy Sunday mornings pottering around the garden or the double garage, or simply lie in a hammock on the patio, nursing a hangover and keeping an eye on my neighbour's wife, scheming how I can manoeuvre her into a situation and position where I can screw her.'

'Whitey!' The expression on Manya's face was one of wide-eyed bewilderment, tinged with horror. And it was a picture of her that he would never forget. Fashioning as serious an expression as was possible on his own face, he hurried on:

'My house in Surburbia will be full of expensive, practically functionless junk and my wife will want more and more of it, because the guy next door is called Jones, and *his* wife has just had a new load of it delivered by the most expensive junk-shop in town.

'As Joe Dokes, I will drink just as much as I do now, but I will do my drinking in posh places like the Country Club and the best hotels, or out on the patio of my ranch-type, jerry-built house, which my wife, goaded on by my mother-in-law, has named 'Mandalay' or 'Linga-Longa' or perhaps that time-honoured perennial 'Shangri-La'. When I get the horries, I will be rushed into an expensive drying-out joint. My colleagues will commiserate with me and my family, because at one time or another, they have been in the same place for the same reason. My staff will be told that poor Mister J.D. is suffering from commercial dyspepsia, or whatever complaint happens to be fashionable in Suburbia at the time. While I am drying-out, Jones my neighbour will have the opportunity for which he has been waiting for a long time: he will be able to manoeuvre *my* wife into a position and situation, where *he* will be able to screw *her*.'

Manya gave a gasp. 'Whitey, that's terrible! I don't know where Suburbia is — I've never heard of it, but I'm sure that all those people who live in those lovely houses, don't act like that.' Her face was quite bleak. His bizarre attempt to be stunningly funny had gone right over her head.

'Of course they don't Manya. I'm sorry if I have been offensive. But as I said earlier, in trying to substantiate my own miserable station in life, I have to rationalize, to feel *somehow* that I am contributing my share to the balance and stability of the population of the globe. The world would be a terrible place in which to live if it were full of guys like Joe Dokes. And it would be even worse if the male population was made up of fellows like me.

How colourless life would be were it nor for the proportionate existence of the good and the bad, the beautiful and the ugly, the steady and the wayward.' He grinned at Manya's serious face. 'Long ago when I was young . . .'

'Whitey you're not *that* old! And I am sure that you don't believe all that nonsense about being a successful failure. You're just using it as an excuse for the bad patch that you've struck. I'm sure that you'll be all right now.'

Here we go again, he thought, but he was happy to see that Manya was smiling again. 'I wish I could share your optimism,' he said softly. 'But it seems that it is my fate to drift down the by-ways of life with the oddballs. And let me say again that I'm not complaining. Look at all the wonderful and curious people that I've met — people of all races, creeds and persuasions: beautiful people full of ugliness; pitiable people abounding in spiritual beauty. If I were Joe Dokes I would never have met you and Mommy and Achmet Smit, and so many others who either accept or reject you for what you are, not for what they, in their selfishness, would like you to be.' Musing on, he thought of Doctor Milly Mayhew and the patient, weary male-nurses in the State Hospital, over-worked but unflagging and unsung.

Manya lay back on the bed, and it seemed to him that she had fallen asleep. Binty lay unstirring in his cot in the soft pink glow of the light. It was time now for him to leave. He stood up and his head and shoulders seemed to disappear into an inky fog; then there was chaos in his head as a searing pain shot through his skull. He heard Manya gasp as he clutched at the edge of the dressing table. Then as quickly as it had descended, the darkness withdrew again. Manya was standing before him, looking at him with alarmed eyes. 'Your eyes are all funny. Do you feel sick?'

Her words reached him from the other side of the world, and there seemed to be an ugly grey wind passing through his head. It's the meths, he thought; then the grey wind moaned a little and died. 'I stood up too quickly,' he said, trying to smile reassuringly, for the girl's eyes were wide with alarm. She stood very close to him, and he lifted one of the heavy, silky black braids. She seemed not to notice the act, and in the heavy silence in the room she continued to look up at him, her eyes searching his face. Suddenly there was a scratching sound, and Manya gave a little cry and moved into his waiting arms. Without thought to consequences, he tilted her face and kissed her soft, parted lips. And he was conscious only of the most sensational display of shooting fireworks. His entire being seemed to erupt and burn away amid multi-coloured sparks and spangles and zinging tracers of jasmine-flavoured fire. Then his heart kicked-over, caught and thumped away again, but he continued to hold her close as she looked up into his face.

'Why did you do that, Whitey?'

'Kiss you?'

'Yes.'

'I don't quite know. But perhaps the explanation is very simple. You are a very desirable woman and I am a man.'

The scratching sound was repeated, then Binty whimpered. Manya tried to draw away from him, but he held her against him. She struggled briefly, still looking up into his face, then she responded and laid her head against his chest.

'Not now, Bokkie,' she said softly. 'I'm so tired. Please let me go.'

He stroked her beautiful black hair for a moment, reason and biological desire raging in conflict across his mind, then he reluctantly dropped his arms.

Binty was sitting up in his cot, his face pressed between two of the bars. Manya attended to the child, settling him down with a bottle, then she returned to stand before him.

'You must go now, Whitey. I am truly very tired, and you look . . . well . . . terrible. Find a quiet corner in the voorkamer and try to rest.' Once again the look of concern appeared in her eyes. 'And Whitey, you mustn't drink any more spirits.'

So much for phoney toothpaste ads, he thought bleakly, feeling rotten and filthy at having been caught out. He walked heavily to the door. 'I'm sorry if I've offended you.'

'Don't worry about that at all . . . Paul. I'll see you in the morning.'

He had the impression that she was about to come towards him. 'Good-bye, Gertie Smit. Thank you for all your wonderful kindness.'

He went out, and though he closed the door quickly, he caught her soft reply:

'Salaam aleikum, Paul.'

8

i

Standing in the dimly-lit passage outside Manya's door, he experienced a moment of truth, almost as if it had been triggered by the sharp snap of her door-latch: what a miserable thing he was! How, as a human being, could he possibly compare himself with the decent and courageous girl beyond that door? Looking towards the smoke-hazy rectangle of the voorkamer, his eyes flickering sporadically under the attack of the meths on his optic nerve, still conscious of the scent of Manya's soft body, he had a sudden desire for normality; just to be a normal man with a normal job, a home and a woman of his own; just to be able to take a few drinks then say, 'That's it,' and go home. The idea was appealing, but only for a moment, then he thought about the dreary past and the even more hopeless future because of the effort required, the so-called will-power that the do-gooders are always spouting about. It was too late now. Fate had cast him in this mould. 'I am what I am.' His shoulders slumped in defeat and resignation.

His physical weariness had increased to a steady throbbing as his body called out for the natural sleep it had been denied by the constant presence of alcohol in his system, allowing the nerves no rest. Even though consciousness had been absent all the long hours of the afternoon and evening, his mind had restlessly expended energy, churning out its forgotten dreams. Straightening his weary shoulders, he walked towards the voorkamer and stood briefly in the doorway.

'Avast, ye bearded vark!'

Ben Gunn's mad black eyes bored into him as he moved into the big room. The old man, who had been asleep at the table when he passed through earlier, was now wide awake, and his six-bottle can was down to about a quarter.

The sextet at one of the smaller tables, the gentoos and the seamen, lapsed into silence as he entered the room; the men eyeing him with suspicion. Two of them were young coloured men, probably of Anglo-African descent, dressed in jeans and bright shirts. The third seaman was a big, middle-aged fair man dressed in a brown suit. The whores, of uncertain ethnic origin, dressed in eye-torturing creations of pink and green finery, looked him over boldly, each obviously trying to decide whether or not he was a better gypping proposition than the bird in hand. The Jesus-girl, whom Manya had mentioned, was not to be seen. In the subdued light of two standard lamps at each end, the voorkamer, hazy with cigarette smoke, seemed lower and more cavernous than he remembered.

' I heed about ye, Whitey,' Ben Gunn said, displaying his blackened broken teeth. 'I heed ye're a drinking man like mesel.' Have a pot o' jupe we'ol Ben. Git yesel' a Khyber.'

'A what?'

'A Khyber, ye thick pig! A Khyber Pass — a glass!'

He grinned at the old man. 'I'm a South African loyal and true,' he said theatrically. 'I'll git mesel' a Sir Lowry's Pass.' On his way to the kitchen he passed one of the foam-rubber couches upon which a pair of gentoos sat playing a waiting game over a single bottle of jupe, displaying their nylon-clad thighs and frilly slips. One of them, agonizingly stuffed into taut black satin, smiled at him as he passed by. 'Hello, Whitey darling,' she said boldly. Bowing briefly, he walked on, but he caught the remark passed by her companion: 'Sy moer, forkkin' witgat.'

In the passage, he bumped into the white girl, who had just stepped out of the bathroom. He stopped and stared at her, fascinated by the beauty of her profile. She was grubby and untidy, festooned with bangles and beads. If she had any breasts at all they were hidden, nun-like, by the garment which clothed her from neck to toe, and which could quite easily be someone's discarded floral curtain. She stood almost on top of him for a moment, and she didn't smell all violets—smelled, in fact, as if she had been living on the outers for a couple of weeks. 'I beg your pardon,' he said, standing aside so that the girl could pass. She looked up at him nervously, then scurried into the voorkamer.

Ou Lem was in the kitchen, hooked on the wild-weed and so drunk that he could hardly support himself against the dresser on which he was hanging with his elbows. Mommy Stilhuis sat in a massive wicker chair, guarding the door of her fake linen-cupboard. 'You look a bit better,' she observed sourly. 'I suppose it's another drink you want now?' Her tone of voice was coarser than he remembered. It was probably the one she adopted when smokkeling.

'Just a glass, Mommy. Old Ben's offered me a pot 'o jupe.'

'Huh, Ben. That Ben. That old vark! He'll get you going again then drink you under the table.' Her eyes narrowed, and she looked at him for a long, searching moment. 'I can see that you've had a few. Remember what I said out there in the yard this morning?

'Just a little ol'drink with Ben, Mommy, that's all. Anyway, I'm a big boy now.'

'Big boy my arse! You drunks are all the same. A few drinks and you're looking for a shoulder to cry on!'

Willy came through a door which led off the kitchen — probably the smokkeling room used at night. Willy was wearing a fighting-belt through the loops of a pair of faded jeans. The young man's eyes were over-bright and insolent, and it was obvious that he had been blowing the weed to some extent. Willy nodded a brief greeting, then went down the passage to the voorkamer, to call loudly for order as a woman's shrill burst of laughter rose above the general subdued drone of voices.

Picking up a glass from the dresser, he glanced at the vertically snoozing ou Lem, then he turned back to Mommy Stilhuis, to thank her for her hospitality, for he felt that she would not be up and about when he left in the morning. And then he stopped and frowned.

The old woman's eyes were fixed on the passage, and a transformation had occurred. The usually hard black eyes were filled with concern, the dark face heavy with brooding worry. Mommy sat for almost half a minute, quite still, seemingly oblivious of his presence a few feet away. At length she blinked her eyes and looked across at him. 'You can see what he has been doing, Whitey,' she said heavily. 'And it is all my fault. I brought him into this world and his future was my responsibility, but now he is slipping away from me and I don't seem to have the strength to hold him back. He is twenty-one and earns enough to support himself. But if he carries on with the wine-swilling and the dagga-smoking, it won't be long before he is in serious trouble. My greatest torment is that he will not listen to reason, though sometimes I must agree when he argues that he is a nothing, as he calls himself, in this world; that at his job he is just 'that scooter boy', whereas his father was *Mister* Stilhuis, the engineer. Even when I tell him to be patient — explain that he is still young — that his working life has just begun, that he has his whole future before him, and that bitterness only poisons the heart, he only scowls and argues that we are nothing, that we have no place on this earth; that heaven is our only home. I don't know where he got this silly idea from — perhaps listening to some gloomy prophet on the street corner. Anyway all that I can do now is to pray to Almighty God, and hope that the peaceful early years that my boys spent in this house with their father will overcome the influence of this place, and that one day our people will be uplifted to dignity and hope.'

The old woman lapsed into silence, and gazed into the middle distance as if the new horizon of which she spoke were there before her mind's eye, and he hoped that she would soon be done with the thing that was on her mind. It was a subject which embarrassed him and which he seldom discussed, for on the low level of society on which he moved there was no room for it: a battler was a battler, irrespective of creed or the colour of his skin.

'My late husband Hans Stilhuis was a Dutch marine engineer, Whitey. He was a hard-working sober man, and he was kind and thoughtful, but trust my luck to marry the only Kaaskop in the world who was not a tightwad. He was the neighbourhood sucker, and he knew it. When he died he left nothing but the furniture in this house. I had three little children and I had to feed them, so I turned to smokkeling. By District Six standards I am a wealthy woman, and I do not see my gains as ill-gotten: if people didn't buy from me they would find the stuff in a dozen other places like this in this area. I have bought a house in Athlone — something that I have dreamed about for years, but I feel somehow that it is too late; that I shall spend my remaining years there, not in peace, but in the agony of knowing that I have failed my boys. If Willy becomes a victim of this way of life, it will be because of my greed: I could have moved out five years ago. I sometimes feel that I am an evil old woman, but I ask God for nothing for myself. I pray only that he should guide my boys.'

He stood there, toying with the glass in his hand and wondering what sort of impression he gave people that they should want to open their hearts to him. Perhaps he was considered so low that he was of little consequence?

In the silence that ensued, Mommy sat still, her hands clasped in her lap, her eyes fixed upon something beyond physical vision, then slowly her face and eyes hardened to their normal appearance. Her profile became firm and stubborn, as if she dared God *not* to guide her boys into a righteous way of life. She turned and looked up at him, and he could see that the thing was all over.

'Have you had a good rest, Whitey?'

'Yes. I slept for a few hours, and I've had a bath and eaten. You have been very kind to me, Mommy.'

'It cost me nothing. What are you going to do now — I mean tomorrow?'

'I'll pull out in the morning and make my way back to East London.'

'All right, if that's the way you feel. But don't get under my feet, and don't cause any bullshit. I have enough on my hands with that Boon.' Heaving herself out of her great basket-chair, she went across to the dresser and dug a vicious elbow into ou Lem's ribs. The skolly grunted and moved aside, sliding limply down on to a stool, where he sat slumped with his chin on his chest.

Mommy took a key from the great bunch at her girdle and unlocked a drawer. She gave him a long, deliberating look, then peeled a five rand note from the biggest choker he had ever seen, and stuffed it into the pocket of his shirt. 'I don't know why I'm stupid enough to give you that, so don't ask. And don't spend it here; you'll need it for the road.' She locked the drawer, and was lumbering back to her chair when Willy came back into the kitchen.

'Vodka for the sailors,' he said, sauntering across the floor. His thumbs were hooked in the waist-band of his jeans, and with his surly face he looked every inch the potential skolly.

Mommy looked at her son and heir, and briefly closed her eyes, as if the sight of him was both painful and disgusting. 'Are they behaving in there?' she demanded.

'They're just joking and playing matches,' Willy said.

'I want them out at twelve o'clock. And I want those other two whores out right now. I've got a feeling about tonight!' She opened her linen-cupboard, which contained a good hundred rand's worth of liquor on the shelves, and cans of sweetwine and jupe on the floor. 'Four-fifty,' she said to Willy, handing him the bottle.

Her son looked at her in some surprise. 'The first two bottles were four rand each, Mommy. They'll argue.'

His mother looked at him coldly. 'That was when they were sober. This one is four-fifty, whether they argue or not. And if they get tough, tell them to take their whores to the Mount Nelson Hotel.'

Willy shrugged and went off, and presently the two girls who had been sitting by themselves came into the kitchen. They looked sullen and annoyed.

'Ons het nie geraas, Mommy,' said one hoarsely.

'We wasn't doing nothing,' pleaded the other, the black-satin one. She was a shapely young girl, but with an acne-pitted face and thin lips. And she was a battler. She winked at him and gave him the nod. Shrugging, he pulled out the linings of his trouser pockets, making his destitution abundantly apparent.

'I know you wasn't making a noise!' Mommy snapped. 'And you wasn't buying either . . . out!'

They moved without hesitation, out of the back door and across the yard. He heard the loud snap of the bolt being drawn, the creak of the gate, and then the hammering sound of the tin as the gate was slammed shut in anger. Mommy seemed unperturbed. She returned to her chair, and reaching down beside it, she came up with a big black leather-bound Bible. She fitted her steel-rimmed glasses, then looked at him over the rims. 'Go talk with Ben, or go to bed!' she snapped. She began to read, and he knew that she had forgotten all about him.

ii

The Limeys and the girls had paired off. Each of the black ones and his girl had taken possession of a couch, and had started the count-down, checking all systems in preparation for the blast-off in whatever sleazy room his girl occupied. The big Limey and the girl of his choice, a thin vicious-looking slut, were still seated at the table, engaged in what seemed to be a serious discussion. There was no evidence that the visitors to South Africa's hospitable shores had found the price of the last bottle of vodka criminally exorbitant. The men were not all that drunk, so very likely they were prepared to pay the cut-throat prices in an illegal house where they could entertain their Coloured girl-friends, thus aiding the archaic liquor laws to defeat their very purpose. The big Limey looked up at him as he drew abreast of the table.

'Hello, lad,' the man said, smiling slowly. 'What about a wee pot?' The man had a big open face and a mashed nose, beneath a thatch of sandy unkempt hair.

He hesitated, and by so doing, he felt somehow that he had lost something. A brief, but terrible conflict occurred in his tired mind, then the big Limey poured a massive slug of vodka into the glass in his hand. 'Cheers, lad,' the man said in his burring North Country accent.

'You speaka da English, George?' A black seaman with a nasty sneering face dug his elbow into the flabby breast of his gentoo and roared with laughter.

'Shoot thy bloody trap!' the big Limey snapped, glaring across at the black man. 'Were ye no taught to be courteous in a furren country?'

'I didn't mean nuffin',' the black Cockney said hurriedly. 'I was just havin' a lark on like, Boats.'

The bo'son fixed the young seaman with a bleary stare, and warned him once again to keep quiet. 'I didn't bring ye here for a lark. I knows this area, and I don't want to have t'carry t'likes o' you back t'ship with t'skin stripped offa ya.' His own voice was over-loud, and he was more sozzled than he had at first appeared to be.

Clutching his half-tumbler of vodka, he grinned from Boats to the black seaman. 'I don't go for stripping the skin off blokes' backs,' he said. 'I'm a seaman, just like you.'

'I didn't mean you,' Boats said. 'And I thought you had t' look of t'sea about ya.' He went on to explain that they were out to paint the town, in a quiet way, after a long stormy voyage from Liverpool, in a Harrison Boat.

'A Harrison Boat? I shipped out to Hong Kong in a Harrison; a long while back, though. One of fat and two of lean, eh.'

Boats grinned. 'Them were t'old days, lad. You couldn't find better living boats than t'Harrison, nowadays.'

'A Harrison, eh. What ship?' The second black seaman, a goodlooking moon-faced boy, untangled himself from his whore, and grinned down the length of the couch. There was a long, timed pause, then the five of them, including Ben Gunn, all roared in unison: HARDSHIP! And another link with the sea was forged. Willy came bounding in, to call for order. But when it was apparent that nothing serious was about to happen, the young man scowled around and went off back to the kitchen.

Chuckling to himself, he looked briefly into the tumbler of neat vodka, and during that infinitesimal fragment of time all thought other than to drink it, was erased from his mind. He gagged and swayed under the impact of the raw spirit striking his stomach. Fighting to keep it down, he accepted a Woodbine and a light from Boats; then waving a hand of farewell to the group in general, and with the knowledge that the vodka had settled, he turned towards the big table and gave his attention to the drinking phenomenon he called Ben Gunn, and the strange-looking young girl, who seemed so out of place in a smokkelhuis. With the impact of the vodka rapidly subsiding, and the glow beginning to spread throughout his system, he pulled out a chair and looked at the youngster, and for the life of him, he was unable to reconcile her arrival with that of the whores and the seamen.

She sat with her elbows on the table, a few feet away from old Ben. Her innocent little face was cupped in her hands, and she flashed him a brief, very nervous smile as he sat down opposite the old man. The girl had probably never had a drink in all her life, and he felt that a good bath, some decent clothes and a few plates of meat and spuds would transform her into a very attractive young lady. However, nothing short of rebirth would transform Ben Gunn.

The old salt's wild, black eyes were embedded in discs of flaming red, but his speech was quite steady and coherent. 'Where ye all from, Whitey?' he asked, reaching for the tumbler and filling it with wine.

He gave the old fellow the spiel about the Land beyond the Midnight Sun and the Sixth Day of Christmas, and for a long moment the mad black eyes crawled over his face, then Ben snorted in disgust. 'Mad as a pig!' he said, addressing the girl, whose little mouth was hanging open, her eyes wide with wonder and fear. Then, in a silvery voice, Ben Gunn added, by way of introduction: 'This is me old mate, Whitey. He's as mad as a vark!' Ben gave a loud burst of obscene laughter. 'Let's splice t'fucking main-brace, me mate!'

Willy came rushing in, to shake the old man by the shoulder. 'Keep quiet, you old bastard. My mommy says any more noise out of you, and out you go — without your wine.' Willy lifted the almost empty can by the ring, and stepped away from the table. 'And my mommy says your money's run out. No more after this.' He gave the old man a sharp cuff on the ear, and replacing the can, he moved off to the kitchen end of the voorkamer, where he stood, arms folded across his chest, glaring around the big room.

The big shot of vodka was wreaking its havoc, dissolving memory and rapidly eroding resolve; evaporating weariness, it shunted him into the slot of the great and glorious *Now!* He grinned at the downcast Ben. 'Cheer-up, old cocker; maybe the Limeys will buy you a pot when your can's finished.'

'Oh, shame,' the girl said with considerable compassion. 'Poor old man.'

But the chastised old man was not to be comforted. Ben sat huddled down in his chair, a picture of insane apathy. Then he began remorsefully to scratch his head, the black nails of his filthy fingers digging into the matted, coir-like hair. After a while he gave his attention to his bearded face, and there were faint smears of pale blood on his tips of his black nails. Presently, having routed whatever it was he had been pursuing, the old man straightened in his chair and leaned forward.

'Did I tell ye about me little bird, Whitey?' he asked in a low whisper, one wild eye, seemingly independent of its mate, swivelling round to where Willy was standing on guard. The wayward eye lingered on the young man for a moment, then returned. 'It's a little yellow bird, Whitey; I call him Tomtit.'

He felt the hair prickling on the back of his neck, and suddenly he was quite cold, though the room was stuffy. He had the urge to remove his eyes elsewhere, or shut them against the crazy face of the old man. However, he felt it prudent to keep them open, and just as ou Lem had done in the presence of the police that morning, he fixed his eyes on the photograph of J. C. Smuts. But after a while, he found that the unsmiling eyes of Slim Jan held a chilly light and little interest in the activities of the common people. Then the old general's thin lips drooped at the corners in a sneer of disgust.

Rattled now, he returned his gaze to the mad face across the table, fixing them on the summit of the hirsute dome. It was scruffy, and he was fascinated by a movement he fancied he saw up there, of a tiny crustaceous creature whose domain is usually the pubic forest to the south. Closing his eyes briefly, he took a long pull on his jupe. 'Tell me about your little bird, Ben,' he said with feigned interest.

What kind is it?' the girl asked eagerly. 'I simply *love* birds and timid creatures!'

Ben turned his head slowly towards the girl and looked at her with devouring eyes. What little colour she had drained from her face. Her hand leaped to her throat and she gave a little gasp. She tried to smile, but it failed completely, and then as if pursued by the devil himself, she leaped up from the table and fled into the bathroom in the passage.

The mad old thing gave a low, crackling laugh and raised his glass to his lips, but without drinking. As if struck by a sudden new thought, he lowered it again. 'What bird; what are ye talking about?' he asked, looking across the table with hate and suspicion in his eyes. So intent and unblinking was his gaze, that his eyes began a rapid though minute flickering from side to side, so that they became horribly hypnotic. Mercifully, it was of short duration; then the eyes took on a sly, cunning expression. 'I knows all about ye, ye bearded vark!' Ben said in a whiplash whisper. 'Ye're trying to get information out of old Ben. But I'll not tell ye what I heed on upper-deck this morning. I'll not tell ye about buzz.'

The cold psychic wind swept through him, and he felt the chill of sweat trickling down his sides. He searched frantically in his mind for something to say that would break the spell that was upon the insane old creature. He knew that the word 'buzz' was the naval one for 'rumour', so whatever it was that Ben had in mind would have something to do with the navy. 'We're going to get a double-tot of neaters, is that it, Ben; is that the buzz, old cocker?'

But Ben, gazing beyond him, seemed not to hear his words. His eyes had grown calm and there was a distant look about them. 'Oh, yes, t'buzz,' he said at length. 'Pour us a gill o'grog, Tommy; and I'll tell ye t'buzz.' There was a long pause while Ben nodded and smiled to himself; then he said, 'Thanke, Tommy. I heed a buzz in t'wardroom pantry this morning, Tommy. I heed that Vice-Admiral Nagumo has brought his First Fleet into t'Indian Ocean. Ye know Vice-Admiral Nagumo, Tommy. Him what did Yanks dirt at Pearl Harbour last December . . .'

If the old man had started to tell him about a little green ship called Tomtit, it would have been easy, he felt, to burst out laughing and get up from the table. But now there was something horrible that rooted him to his chair as he listened to the clear calm voice, the voice of a young man in the prime of life; perhaps a seaman-gunner at action stations in the turret of a speeding, fighting cruiser, his thoughts suddenly trapped by shock for thirty years or more in a bubble of lucid sanity in the psychotic froth of his brain.

With his damp palms pressed against the table, he tried to rise, but found that he had not the strength. Then the voice in Ben Gunn spoke again.

'Do ye think that Nagumo will beat us, Tommy me lad? He sank *Dorsetshire* and *Cornwall* last week; on Easter Sunday, it were, I heed. A great shame that they sent they two ships south from Colombo, when they knowed what was waiting somewhere down there: three fleet-carriers and battle-waggons the size o' Battersea Power Station, and heavy cruisers and destroyers. Terrible, I heed it were; on a bright, calm day with visibility as far as forever. Wonder why *'Shire* and *Cornwall* didn't make smoke and run back into it, Tommy? Not much hope in it, but it would have given gunners time to get t'sun out o' they eyes and dry they arses. Took all o' eight minutes to finish ol *'Shire,* I heed, Tommy . . .'

There was a low buzzing sound in his head, and he grew more terrified with the realisation that perhaps the vlam and the vodka had completed their ugly work, and that his mind had finally cracked; that perhaps Ben Gunn wasn't talking at all, but that the voice was in his own head . . .

'Heed they little yellow shitballs in they aeroplanes dropped out o' t'sun when t'gunners were blinded by it, Tommy. Heed they had no hope, and *'Shire's* turrets were trained this hopeless way and that; they great, proud guns what had helped to finish *Bismarck,* blasted and hanging down like t'trunks o' dying hefferlants, t'little yellow shitballs leaning out o' they cockpits, taking pictures like they was flying o' er Blackpool of a Bank Holiday — ahhhh . . .' Ben Gunn gave a long painful sigh, before continuing.

'Heed they chiefs and petty-officers down below refused t'believe t'order to abandon ship. And t'little Royal Marine bugle-boy, trapped in t'twisted Control-Top, crying his eyes out for shame, and sounding his last 'Retreat' on his bright brass bugle, and only a paltry shot or two fired in all the action. Heed they dropped oil-bombs on poor ol' dying *'Shire,* did hon'rable little yellow shitballs, Tommy. Heed they lads on upper-deck was burned something terrible, they skin hanging from they limbs like strips o' pale silk, and they fallin' in t'hoggin' in screaming dying agony. Thirty-one hours I heed they lads was in t'hoggin', with nowt but flotsam and *'Shire's* old wooden masts t'hold to, and t'terrible sun burning down and t'Noah's Arks cruising around at dorsal depth, all the while. And not a complaint out o' they brave singing lads all t'long day and night, Tommy. *Enterprise* and two destroyers I heed it were what picked up t'lads at sunset of a Monday evening, with t'sea getting up and t'sharks moving in to snap up they glad stragglers . . . ahhhhh, Tommy; two great ships and four-hundred and twenty men lost in t'deep . . .'

For the past thirty seconds, his eyes had been screwed up tight, and he found that he had no desire to open them. The spectral young voice from the impossible past had trailed-off, and now there were only the sounds and the low voices of the people in the room to be heard. And then, from across the table, the voice of Ben Gunn, low and hardly audible. The old man was singing softly an old English melody which some modern naval laureate had adapted for a canteen sing-song:

> I was walking through the dockyard in a panic,
> when I met a sailor old and grey.
> On his shoulder was his kit-bag and his hammock,
> and this is what I heard him say:
> 'Oh I wonder, yes I wonder
> if the Jaunty made a blunder
> when he made this draft-chit out for me.
> Oh I've been a barrack stanchion,
> and I've lived in Drake's old mansion
> and I always say good-morning to the Chief.
> 'Good-morning, Chief!'
> Oh I wonder, yes I wonder
> if the Jaunty made a blunder,
> when he sent this old man off . . . to . . . sea?'

The soft, broken sounds died away. He could hear the voices of Boats and his gentoo in low, muzzy argument. Then there were sudden giggles, the smacks of wet kisses, chuckles and snatches of pop songs from the direction of the couch occupied by the young seamen and their girls, and then, from across the table, snivelling and sniffing sounds. Opening his eyes, he was shocked to see that Ben Gunn was weeping.

The fear within him drained away, leaving only the shame that it should have been there at all. Reaching for the can, he poured two full glasses, which left about an inch of wine in the bottom. 'Cheers, Ben,' he said brightly. 'Down the hatch, old cocker!' And down it went, to pacify the raging ache in his guts. He pushed up from the table, to wobble a little on his legs.

For a bewildered moment the old man looked up at him and then down at the glass in his hand, as if surprised to find it there. 'Don't go, Whitey,' he whined. 'I want to tell ye about me little dog . . .' Ben Gun had returned from the past as mad as ever.

Moving away from the table, he found that something was nagging at his mind. Was it somewhere he had to go to; something he ought to do quite urgently? He struggled with the problem for a long moment, but it slipped away, leaving him vaguely uneasy. He cadged a smoke from Boats, who pushed the packet across without looking up. It seemed that the argument the man was having with his gentoo was a heated one about some money that had gone missing on a previous trip to Cape Town.

In the act of returning the cigarettes and matches to the table, he stopped and gazed around the room, for he had caught the sound of the whirring of tiny wings. He listened carefully with his inner ear. 'Catch a knock,' the tiny voice said. He smiled to himself, and the nagging in his mind was gone. Picking out a couch in a gloomy corner of the voorkamer, he headed towards it, and then bumped into Eddie, who had just come into the room.

The boy looked around warily, then attacked the radiogram. Deftly slipping a disc from its sleeve, he dusted it on the seat of his trousers. In a trice he had it on the turntable, and presently the powerful, driving voice of Tom Jones bemoaned the infidelity of his 'bird' Delilah. Blessedly, in deference to the late hours and the company, the boy lowered the volume. Then, apparently somewhat appeased, Eddie smiled his dazzling smile. 'You look okay now, Whitey,' he said. 'But I can see that you've got a lekker pot in you.'

Which was very true. The brief spell of fear-induced sobriety he had experienced whilst seated with Ben Gun, had ended. 'I feel fine and dandy, Eddie,' he said, wondering why he had said it, for he was feeling most peculiar. 'How was the movie?'

Eddie started in on the film-story.

And he felt trapped. He had expected a simple 'good' or 'lousy' verdict from the boy. But no! He had to endure the painfully long recounting of the entire horse-opera, told in the rapid, colourful idiom of District Six. And he was feeling very odd and faraway. He stood looking down at the spinning disc, listening with half an ear, while he watched his mind wandering off to that strange region on the edge of amnesia. The soulful music and the record revolving through shafts of vagrant light had a deeply soothing, hypnotic effect on his consciousness. Eddie's voice and the crack of the six-gun he made with his lips receded to a point beyond audibility. Looking up, he saw that the boy's mouth was moving; his facial expressions were animated and vivid, but there was no sound.

Across the room, Boats had his gentoo on his lap. Her arms were flung around his neck, and her mouth was wide with vulgar laughter, but there was no sound. Fear was edging in, and he dug his nails into the palms of his hands and shook his head violently, and the sound came rushing back, as if plugs had been suddenly pulled from his ears.

. . . toe skit die cowboy die skelem in sy forkin' moer, en vat die meisie terug *ranch* toe.' Eddie was smiling with pleasure. 'It was a lekker fliek, Ou Whitey. Shooo, but he was a bad rustler, that vark, ek sê, ou Whitey!'

Eddie's smile faded quite suddenly, and he assumed, at first, that it was because of the boy's dislike of the celluloid crook, but Eddie was looking beyond him, towards the kitchen, and turning slowly, he saw a great tall black man standing in the passage doorway, blocking it completely. The giant took a step into the voorkamer, and behind him in the gloomy passage stood Willy, his studded belt slung over his shoulder. Bringing up in the rear of Willy, his face tight and evil-looking, was Boon.

'Hy's Mule, ou Whitey,' Eddie whispered in his ear. 'Hy's baie gevaarlik.'

And this Mule certainly looked dangerous. The giant black man wore a filthy singlet and a pair of ragged jeans, which reached only to his bulging calves, and were obscenely tight at the greasy bulging crotch. The eyes in the great glistening face were wild and red-rimmed with drink, and the tunnels of the nostrils flared like those of a startled stallion as Mule stared around the room, as if seeking the thing which had startled him. Then he advanced into the voorkamer, bringing with him the violent odour of Africa.

The sharp 'click' of the record-player switching off brought him out of the trance of fear, and he moved back against the heavy dresser, his right hand close to one of the Bali heads, for at this late hour, he had no desire to be mangled by a pissed-up, seven-foot gorilla.

'Avast, ye black pig!' Ben's sudden wild hail rang around the room, shattering the silence. 'Come and have a pot o' jupe we'ol Ben!'

Mule stopped for a moment, then moving unsteadily, he sat down opposite the old salt, placing his sweaty ham-like arms on the table. The giant's face was bemused and slack and his eyes rolled alarmingly in his drunkennes, and although he presented a frightening, primitive picture, he evinced neither malice nor hate, but something pitiable and degraded.

Ben chuckled with a sort of evil, malicious glee. With his mad black eyes fixed on Mule's face, he pointed a long filthy finger, and began to chant the ludicrous jingle which sprang from the Deep South during the shameful era of human slavery:

God made da'nigger
He made him in da'night
He made him in a hurry
And forgot to paint him white!

The jingle was followed by Ben's insane, mocking laughter, and out of appreciation, perhaps, Mule showed his great slab teeth in a ghastly grimace; then he reached across and took Ben's can in one massive hand. With the neck of the can in his blubbery mouth, Mule began to drink. There was perhaps two-thirds of a pint left in the can, but the level dropped rapidly to zero, and Ben, his eyes bulging with fury and unreasonable hate, screamed a string of curses and hurled his glass into Mule's face. The heavy tumbler bounced off the broad nose, leaving a livid gash, bounced to the floor and tinkled into fragments, and the tinkling was the only sound in the freezing tension in the room.

The whores had broken their arm-locks on the seamen and their faces were sharply etched with fear in the shaded light. Boats and his woman were motionless: a tableau of alarm.

And now, in the passage doorway, arms akimbo, the massive face as expressionless as a brownstone cliff, stood Mommy Stilhuis, flanked by Willy and the evilly smiling Boon. The skolly and his apprentice had hold of their belts by the tongue-end, and were flicking them eagerly.

Mule's face still carried the twisted grin. So drunk was he now that he seemed unaware of the wound and the blood that was oozing from it. A little stream trickled down his face and mixed with the saliva and wine at the corners of his mouth, dripping steadily from his chin to the green-baize cloth.

Then the expression on Mule's face gave way to childish hurt and sorrow as he let go of the empty can, wiped his hand across his face and saw the blood. 'Ow, baas,' he lamented, looking across at Ben, who was still mumbling away. 'Ow, ow!' Tears welled-up in the red-rimmed eyes; then, as if stirred by some deep-seated, primitive impulse, Mule reached out across the table, slowly, almost lazily, and took Ben's scrawny throat in one massive hand.

Before anyone could intervene, Mule gave a quick squeeze and shook the old man like a terrier shakes a rat. Ben was lifted off his feet, his eyes bulging alarmingly, and the length of his tongue sticking out of his mouth would have done justice to any self-respecting aardvark. The high, silent tension in the room was broken by a yell from the big Limey. 'He's strangling t'oud lad! For Christ's sake let's do something!'

What was to be done? Only one thing that he, standing against the dresser a few feet from Mule's back, could think of. He picked up the Bali head to bring it down on Mule's arms, to break the strangle-hold, when suddenly he was thrust aside, and a vicious belt-buckle whistled past his face; then another and yet another. He stumbled back, out of range of the flailing belts. Then Mommy, moving with astonishing speed, smashed bodily into the still seated, cowering Mule, sending him crashing to the floor amidst the wreckage of the chair.

The poor creature got to his knees, his arms crossed over his head in an effort to protect it against the murderous brass buckles of Willy, Boon, and a remarkably wide-awake ou Lem. With the belts striking in swift, merciless order: Willy, Boon, ou Lem, Willy, Boon, ou Lem, the skollies beat Mule to the floor again, where he thrashed about, trying powerfully to rise. Then, changing his tactics, his face like so much raw liver, Mule began to crawl towards the rear passage.

The big room was in an uproar. The two black seamen and their gentoos were standing on the couch, the better to see, and Ben Gunn was reeling about drunkenly, a hand clutched to his bruised throat. The big Limey called Boats rushed forward. 'Leave t'boyo be!' he yelled. 'Leave him be, he's had enough!' Boon whirled on the big Limey, threatening him with his belt. The skolly's face was livid with naked violence. *'Fuck you!'* he screamed, sending the buckle whistling past the big Limey's agitated sweating face.

Mule was still moving. The giant black man clawed his way up the frame of the passage doorway, and stood swaying on his feet, and the belters moved in, working his body over. The sharp buckles shredded his bloody singlet, and great weals appeared on his broad, black back. Then, when it seemed that Mule was about to collapse, a clear, bell-like, terrified voiçe rang high above the general din. *'Stop it!* Oh, please stop it. You awful ugly people!' The Jesus-girl shot out of the passage and stood with her back to the swaying Mule, her arms spread in an attitude of protection, like a diminutive guardian angel. Her face was colourless, almost translucent in her terror. A whistling buckle caught her a glancing blow on the shoulder, but she seemed not to feel it. 'You awful wicked people!' she cried. 'You are doing this to Jesus, not to this man. Shame on you! Shame, shame . . .' Her eyes rolled back and Boats caught her and lowered her to the floor, where she lay like a rag-doll discarded by some giant child.

The heat was off; the thing was done. All gathered together, the whores and the seamen and Eddie, his young face grey with horror, and Ben Gunn, dancing around and waving his empty can, calling for the death of 'the thieving, black sod'.

The group moved into the kitchen, following Mule's tottering progress to the back door, where the black man turned slowly, his face a sickening sight. The left eye was almost closed, while the other was lost in a gory socket. His arms and hands were slimy with his own blood. His slack, blubbery mouth was mashed, and he began to whimper like a terrified child as Mommy moved towards him. 'Get out!' the old woman snarled. 'I've told you before not to come to my place and make trouble.'

Mule turned away, and with a little animal-like cry, he moved in a staggering run across the yard.

9

i

In the kitchen, the seamen and their girls were gathered in a group, the gentoos clacking away like harpies, carmine talons fluttering at powdered throats, rapacious eyes gleaming with the violence that was past.

'Got his just deserts, t'nigger,' the big Limey said emphatically. 'Drank all t'oud chap's wine, and was intending to strangle him to boot. Can't trust African savages to behave, you can't. Cut your throat for a tanner, t'boggers would!'

His compatriots, their faces gleaming with the sweat of fear, were in instant agreement as they cast fearful glances across to where Willy, Boon and ou Lem were flicking playfully at each other with their belts.

The babble of voices with their strange mixture of accents, both English and Afrikaans, almost drowned Mommy's call for order as she began herding them out of the kitchen. Boats called for a bottle of vodka, and in the voorkamer, the gentoos with the compassion of their kind were gathered around the Jesus-girl, rubbing her frail little wrists and wiping her face with a damp towel fetched from the bathroom. Finally, she was led to a couch and given a glass of water. She seemed none the worse for her courageous defence of Mule, but occasionally she rubbed her shoulder.

When all but Mommy had returned to the voorkamer, and the skollies had gone into the smokkeling-room, he slipped out to the yard, to feel the cool breeze on his sweat-damp body. Dragging the old bench into the deeper gloom beneath the lychee-tree, he sat with his back to the house, facing the flood-lit mountain which brooded above the city. The moon cast a soft light across the poor yard of La Residence Stilhuis, while the old ones lay sleeping behind the darkened windows of their shabby rooms.

Willy came out of the house and crossed the yard to the gate. The young man looked into the lane, then closing the gate he shot the bolt into position, poked his head into the awful goat-shed of a room, then returned to the house.

Sitting almost invisible in the shadow of the tree, he considered the day and the happenings thereof, and was filled with sadness. What a wonderful fair-minded alluring world! The low laugh which escaped his lips was not a bitter one, for he felt that it was not that God had died or gone away, as a great many moderns would have it, but that man had failed his Creator, spurned His love and shattered His Commandments.

The recent violence had reduced his nerves to a jangling cow-bell state, and the thought of returning to the house and going to bed was appalling; the very idea of closing his eyes was terrifying. He would sit it out until the morning. What a pity he had not thought to bring the bottle of vlam with him. Watching the curiously moving patterns of shadow and light created by the foliage of the tree on the grey floor of the yard, he began to muse in a muzzy fragmentary sort of way: substance and shadow — reality and illusion. *Reality* and *illusion?* 'I think, therefore I am'. Therefore by the same token last week I was not, for I did not think. What a reprehensible misnomer! *Pardon, Monsieur Descartes,* all last week I was not, yet I travelled nine-hundred miles! True or false? *True!* If not then I am in East London and all this is an illusion. But it is not an illusion — ask Mule! What is truth anyway — words, words, words!

He laughed again, and listened to the echoes scurrying like fleeing mice into the corners of the yard, while he thought about a drink. The big Limey had called for a bottle of vodka, but the hell with the big Limey; the ignorant two-faced racialist; there was the lovely bottle of vlam in the bathroom. He chuckled as he was struck by a new thought: Ah, I have it, noble Pilate — *vlam et veritas!*

The inane chuckle froze on his lips as a movement in the deep shadowy overhang of the rooms near the gate caught his eye. Something was there on the ground; a long, unmoonlit thing! The sweat of deep fear stood out all over his body, chilly in the night air. With his eyes fixed on the thing, he listened. Creeping across the yard came a sound: the weeping, moaning sound of a soul cast into a medieval hell. Then the long unmoonlit thing became a mound, grew long to some six-feet erect, moved slowly, weeping and moaning towards the gate. He leaped fearfully to his feet as the harsh sound of the gate-bolt cut across the yard, then Mule — or his unhappy wounded ghost — staggered into the lane beyond. In a miasma of sweat-stink, he sank back to the bench, and for many minutes he sat jangling and shaking.

Presently, a dark bank of cloud, travelling before a freshening south-easter, wedged itself between the beaming moon and Signal Hill, and the yard became possessed of a secret darkness, pregnant with the stirrings of night-things: disincarnate things of evil which, it is said, gloat around abattoirs, thrilled to frenzy by the anguished cries of mentally tortured beasts, and the smell of death and blood; things which it is said, lurk around low bars, dives and brothels, seeking to return to the corporeal plane in the smoky, unprotected aura of some sensitive drunk, to experience again and again the lusts and high sensations of the flesh.

The sweat trickling down his sides grew icy as a low tortured groan carried to his ears, and he began to gibber softly as the back gate opened wider, and a patch of white appeared in the dark gap. Then there was a further groan as the gate closed again, and he heard the slow approach of dragging footsteps. The patch of white grew ever closer, and he cowered back fearfully in the deep shadow at the foot of the tree. He closed his eyes, and purple vlam phantoms leaped into his mind, adding to the terror that was already there, increasing the tension to scream-pitch. Placing his hands over his eyes, he peeped through his fingers, and after a moment he gasped in utter relief as he recognised the white jacket, topped by a fez set at a jaunty angle. 'Achmet Smit,' he called breathlessly.

The old man stopped and peered round about. Eventually he came up, his eyes alight with pleasure. The weariness which had caused his dragging footsteps seemed to lift, and the crescent-shaped grin split his face. 'Ha, it is you, ou matroos. You look fine. I see that you have a shirt, and sandals, nogal!'

'I got them from the girl — your daughter. She has been very kind to me. How are you, Achmet Smit; did you walk all the way from the Foreshore?'

The old man sank wearily to the bench and gave a heavy sigh. 'No, I didn't walk. Luckily Mister Tom Maketzi came into the kafee at closing time, and he gave me a lift up here. He dropped me at the lane, and now he has gone in to see Mommy.' The old man rubbed the thin shanks of his legs. 'Shooo, but it has been a day, ou matroos! Today, we sold over sixty chickens and almost a hundred pies!' He cocked his head, and there was a hard proud, business-like gleam in his old eyes. 'Not bad, eh — good business?'

Thankful for the company of the old man, he felt his spirits rising. 'Excellent! The people must have been very hungry today, Achmet Smit?'

'It was the English sailors who were hungry. They must have been drinking beer by the gallon in die Kaap. We also had many songs in the kafee — and two fights.'

'You mean navy sailors?'

'Yes, bluejackets. There are two English warships in the Duncan Dock.' The old man laughed and slapped his knee, and a lascivious glint appeared in his eyes. 'It will be cunt for all in die Kaap, tonight, and then in nine months' time we'll have more babies to look after.'

The old man spoke without rancour, in a matter of fact way, as if the inevitable arrival of a few more of God's little souls like Binty and Cookie was part of the life-style of District Six.

'Who is Tom Maketzi, Achmet Smit?'

'Oh, he's an old friend of Mommy. I believe that he owns a store in Johannesburg. When he comes to die Kaap on business, he always visits with Mommy. I understand that he is very rich. Look, Mister Maketzi bought me a big box of cigarettes!'

Slitting the seal of the box, the old man offered it across, and they lit up and sat blowing smoke into the darkness. It was wonderfully fresh in the yard, with an occasional hair-ruffling south-easterly gust. His nerves had settled down somewhat, but he was conscious of the steadily mounting compulsion. But of the moment, it was by no means critical, and he was unafraid, for he knew that he had only to visit the bathroom, pour a hooker of vlam, and the mysterious desire would be temporarily checked. Nevertheless, there was a vague feeling of apprehension. Experience had taught him that vlam was a double-edged weapon; while it dispersed the old jim-jams quicker than ethyl-alcohol, sudden and extended withdrawal from it was inclined to make Dante's *Inferno* seem like *A Midsummer's Night Dream*.

Beside him on the bench Achmet Smit was slumped like an inert puppet. The old man's chin was on his breast, his cigarette smouldering forgotten between his fingers. The old chap made the faintly bubbling sound of the old when asleep. And from beyond the yard came the nocturnal sounds of District Six: voices raised in song; loud greetings and curses hurled from one dimly-lit street corner to the next; the sudden crash of a wine bottle thoughtlessly tossed from an upper window, and that indefinable sound: an harmonic woven into the tapestry of hope and joy, sorrow and anguish, the laughter and tears of people for whom life is a precious gift to be lived to the fullest possible extent.

He found that his mind was drifting off to Manya in her roseate room. The disturbing feeling he had had when he first saw the girl was upon him again. But now it was bitter-sweet: the sort of feeling an urchin might experience as she gazes at a beautiful doll in the window of a shop.

'*Yissis!*' Achmet Smit gave a loud cry as he tumbled from the bench to land on all fours.

He helped the old man to his feet, a groggy figure with the fez tipped over his eyes. 'I was fast asleep, ou matroos,' he said, grinning sheepishly. 'I was having a lekker dream about a full can of sweetwine.' As if struck by a happy thought, the old man brightened a little. 'I think I still have a little something for us, old friend. I will yust go and check, né.' He moved off towards his room, a bow-legged weary little man nearing the end of a long, long road. He spent almost a full minute fumbling with the padlock, then went inside, and presently the soft glow of a candle appeared at the window.

The moon found a ragged hole in the creeping bank of dark cloud, and its pale light splashed across the yard, starkly etching the edges of the junk and fashioning long spectral fingers and checked patterns of shadow on the grey floor. The south-easter which had threatened to make life miserable had completely died away, and there was a period of quiet, for it seemed that the carousing element of the District had drunk itself to sleep.

It seemed to him that Achmet Smit was a long time in returning, and he gazed anxiously towards the room. He could discern no movement, and after a further minute of waiting he stood up slowly, expecting the phantom with the ice-pick to strike at any moment, but there was only a rising and slowly subsiding wave of dizziness as he walked towards the yellow light in the window. In the room, he found the old fellow lying on his bed — fully clothed, his fez tipped over his eyes. With a small crescent of a smile on his face, Achmet wheezed gently — dead to the world, no longer disturbed by the coughing of his tubercular woman.

Looking down at the sleeper he felt that he would probably never see him again, and the thought saddened him, for his brief association with the old cook of the *Erica* had added to the sum total of his experience. Snuffing the candle, he gently closed the door and went back to the bench.

ii

Through the kitchen doorway he could see Mommy seated at the kitchen table. The old woman was talking to a short, thick-set black man, presumably the businessman from Johannesburg. In a mood of utter weariness and detachment, he watched the pantomime of movements and gestures of the two people framed by the bright rectangle of the doorway. No-one else appeared in his line of vision, and it seemed that full order and a measure of peace had returned to La Residence Stilhuis. Perhaps he ought to go in now, for he was beginning to shiver and rattle as the reaction of the long terrible day beset him, and his earlier decision to sit it out until daylight no longer seemed a good idea. And if he fell into a coma on the bench he would probably be a corpse in the morning. He wondered vaguely if Achmet Smit would mind if he crept in and shared the big bed? He was thinking more seriously about such a move when the Jesus-girl appeared in the doorway.

She stood hesitantly on the step gazing around as if seeking an avenue of escape; then she started towards the gate. Mommy and the black man were staring perplexedly towards the doorway. The girl drew abreast of the bench, and he called out, just loud enough not to startle her. 'Hey. You mustn't go out there. Come over here.'

She swung round, stopped and stood rigid. 'Who . . . who is it?' she gasped.

'Don't be afraid. I'm the man you bumped into in the passage, earlier.'

The girl came slowly towards the bench. A few feet away, she stopped and peered at him. Her eyes were huge and frightened in the pale oval of her face, and her long untidy blonde hair shimmered faintly as she moved her head. 'Oh yes, I remember you . . . Whitey. You were talking to that awful old man.'

'That's right. Sit down here.'

She seated herself at the other end of the bench. Then after a moment, peering fearfully around the ghostly yard with its lunar-like piles of scrap, and perhaps feeling it prudent, she moved up quite close. 'I'm so frightened of those awful ugly people I don't know what to do,' she said in a soft, urgent whisper.

'How on earth did you get to a place like this?'

'I wanted to get to a friend in Rondebosch,' she hurried on in her halting, whispery way. 'I was hitching outside the City Hall . . . in Darling Street . . . oh I'm a fool . . . I'll never hitch at night again . . . this car stopped . . . a cab really . . . and this crowd said jump in . . . those men in there . . . they seemed nice at first . . . then they picked up those awful women . . . instead of turning along Sir Lowry's Road . . . they came up here . . . all jammed in the cab . . . what was I to do . . . big joke!'

He smiled to himself. 'Well, they're seamen, and they get a little carried away when they hit port after a long voyage. I'm sure they never intended to harm you . . .'

'But it was *so* scary! And then the way those others beat that poor harmless man. Oh, Whitey, I'm so afraid. Won't you please take me away from this awful place? It is so late, and my friend Myra will be *terribly* worried!'

'No-one here will harm you. What's your name?' He spoke slowly and gently, trying to soothe her, and in her curious mercurial way her spirits seemed to improve. Her face lit up with pleasure.

'I'm *Flower* today,' she said with a bright smile.

'Oh?' Watching her closely, he noticed that she was relaxing. A little colour had appeared in her formerly wan cheeks, and she had stopped fidgeting with the many strings of beads which hung down over her flat chest. 'Flower. That's a very pretty name. But why only today?'

'Well there's no point in having the same name all your life, is there? I mean, we're never the same from one day to the next, are we? Our names should reflect our spirituality of the day and the way we convey it to other people. I bet your name's not really Whitey . . . it doesn't suit you at all at the moment.' She studied him for a long moment. 'You seem to be sort of vague . . . shadowy . . . *Shadow!*'

'You might have something, Flower,' he said, thinking of Gertie-Manya. 'What was your name yesterday?'

Her little face clouded over. 'Smoky,' she said. 'All last week I was Smoky, because I was *so* sad.'

He knew that the only way to handle this situation was to play along with it. Flower-Smoky was gentle and sweet, and he found that her presence and chatter kept at bay the dark thoughts stirring in his mind. He chuckled softly. 'And tomorrow? What will your name be tomorrow?'

'Tomorrow, Shadow? Tomorrow is only a dream. But if I *should* wake up, then I hope I'll be pretty; then I'll be Rainbow.' She sighed and looked away into the distance. 'I haven't been Rainbow for *such* a long time.'

'I think you're pretty now, Flower. It'll soon be tomorrow, and then I shall call you Rainbow.'

She reached out and touched his hand. 'Thank you for saying that, Shadow. You are kind. You have like sweet, soft vibes.' She continued to look at him in her candid way, then she said, 'Can I come and sleep at your place tonight? It's so late, and I'll never get to Rondebosch at this hour.'

He found something chilling and sad about the new name that Flower had given him. Perhaps in some mystical way she saw him as a shadow of the man he might have been. 'I have no place either, Flower,' he said softly.

'Really! Oh, I feel so sorry for you, Shadow,' she said, sniffling a little. 'It's such a hateful ugly world.'

'Where have you been living then?'

'Oh, we had a place up in Jamieson Street, in Gardens . . . but the police found out where we were . . . started to worry us. It was terrible the way they worried us, Shadow. Every day and night . . . almost they used to come and kick our things around . . . search the cats for dagga . . . call us rubbish, and say nasty things to us. Then the other day they came again. We weren't bothering a soul in the world . . . just sitting around in the sun . . . stringing beads to sell for food . . . when they came barging in. My friend and me were holding hands and talking about Jesus . . . that's all. My friend is a sort of Indian cat . . . and they came in and started on him . . . kicked him in a terrible place . . . I wouldn't even tell you where they kicked my friend. So we decided to go away . . . but we haven't been able to find another place . . . just here there and everywhere.'

'But haven't you any parents or relations?'

Flower sighed. 'No. I'm a sort of orphan. You see, Shadow, my beautiful mother died two years before I was born . . .'

'She did?'

'Yes. Then my father married this other woman who gave birth to me. And she *hated* me!'

'Oh I'm sorry about that, Flower.' The situation was strangely unreal. The clouds had passed away and the drab yard was bathed in silent moonlight. The branches of the lychee-tree were still, yet the leaves whispered. It seemed to him that with the new name she had given him, he and this strange young girl were detached from the world of mortals, were simply projections like the moon shadows webbed on the floor of the yard.

'And I've always been so lonely, Shadow.'

'I think I know how you feel, kid. I know that sort of lost and empty feeling that's inside you. How old are you?'

'I'll soon be eighteen.'

He doubted it, and it seemed to him that she straightened her shoulders and hooded her eyes in an effort to appear older. 'You know if you keep on in this drifting direction you've got a long drag ahead of you,' he said kindly. 'And believe me there will only be greater insecurity and deeper hopelessness as you grow older. To be really happy a person must be functional and useful. I'm no philosopher, but I know that contentment is relative to purpose and action . . .'

'Oh Shadow you've spoiled our lovely association! I didn't ask to be born, but since I *was* born it's my life. People are always telling me what to do with my life, and now you're sounding off at me.'

'Not really, Flower. Everyone has the right to live their own life — do their own thing. I am merely trying to point out that yours might be the wrong thing.' He grinned and patted her shoulder, and taking the five-rand-note from his pocket he put it in her hand. 'There, you take that. Buy some food and get yourself cleaned up, and on Monday go and see the Department of Labour. Try that for a 'thing', just for me.'

'Oh Shadow, you're such an unugly person. I'll write a poem about you some day. Do you like poetry?'

Vaguely uneasy about the situation, he closed his eyes and the wild purple vlam phantoms returned. As the sweat seeped from his body he cowered back in the cold reaches of the shell of fear. Desperately he clutched the edge of the bench, digging his nails into the splintery wood. For a long moment he sat rigid, then slowly warmth and light returned.

'I'm doing my Gospel series of poems at the moment . . . you look funny, Shadow . . . all sweaty . . . do you feel sick?'

'No. Just tired.' Fearfully praying for just a little more time, he watched Flower scratching around in the large patch-pocket of her shapeless gown. She found a little beaded purse, in which she stowed the five-rand-note. Then she produced a shabby jotter which she opened and handed across. Holding the jotter up to the moonlight, he felt the hair prickling on the back of his neck, for both pages of the open book appeared to be blank. But as amnesia receded and he grew calmer, his eyes adjusted to the bad light and he was able to read the almost microscopic script:

They walked the shores of Galilee,
Those good cats.
Twelve minus one.
Following like, the Vortex-Man
Called Jesus,
And blew their minds!

'I'll do the one about you tomorrow,' Flower said, taking the book and stowing it back in her pocket. 'Do you like my work, Shadow?'

The cold spell of unreality was slow in passing and he found it difficult to breathe evenly as his mind nagged away at the bottle of meths in the bathroom. He knew that very soon he would have to make an excuse to go back into the house.

'Well? You're very *dreamy* all of a sudden. *Do* you like my work?'

'I think I do. I was thinking that you're a funny cute little girl. I would like to make a pet of you, but I haven't the time — I think I've used it all up.'

Flower pouted. 'I don't feel cute. I'm still very frightened. I'm always sort of frightened about something; right deep down inside me, and I can't dig it out.' She was silent for a long moment, then she said. 'Could you get me a Coke from these people, Dreamy?' Her eyes were huge and child-like, and there was a pale smile on her lips. 'Please, Whitey-Shadow-Dreamy.'

Looking towards the kitchen, he saw that Mommy and her friend were still seated at the table. Mommy had a cup-and-saucer in front of her, and Tom Maketzi was pouring a beer. Recalling that the rich businessman had given Achmet Smit a lift, he wondered if he might arrange something for Flower before he blacked-out. District Six was no place for a young girl to be at this time of the night. 'If I can get you to Rondebosch will your friend give you a kip?'

Flower nodded eagerly. 'Of course. But how am I to get there?'

'All right, you wait right here.' He stood up slowly, feeling the soundless creaking of his bones. 'Wish me luck. Rainbow.' And to himself he added: *Please God, just a little more time.*

Arranging his clothing and running a hand through his hair, he started towards the house. Half-way to the back door it hit him, and he knew that he had not started a moment too soon. His legs were like jelly and practically out of control. He went reeling forward, to clutch at the doorjamb. Fighting desperately to compose his features, he entered the kitchen, knowing full well that the expression on his face could only be a green and sickly smile.

Mommy Stilhuis was in quite a jovial mood. The old woman obviously enjoyed the company of her friend Tom Maketzi. '*So!* You've been out in the fresh air for quite some time, Whitey,' she said with a grin. 'It's good to take a break now and then, nè?'

He looked at Maketzi, who inclined his head slightly in greeting, the black eyes behind the thick lenses shrewdly appraising, though giving no hint of any decision. Tom Maketzi was broad and tubby and about sixty years old, with an iron-grey cap of hair fitting a high domed head. A grandfatherly figure, Tom Maketzi looked like a shrewd Soweto businessman.

Taking a firm purchase on the end of the table, he looked from one brown face to the other, explaining Flower's predicament and requesting the assistance of Tom Maketzi and his motor-car. 'The child is here by misadventure and she's very frightened,' he managed to say quite firmly. 'She is out there in the yard.' Then he felt himself moving out of the perpendicular. His mind expanded and contracted alarmingly as he heard himself say, 'My name's Whitey-Shadow-Dreamy and I am an alcoholic ...' Whatever else he said thereafter was not registered on his consciousness.

iii

He was standing at the farther end of the passage, looking into the voorkamer. It was empty and silent, reeking with the violence that was past. Three empty vodka-bottles stood on the small table, and Ben's can lay overturned on the floor beneath the table. The smoke from a forgotten cigarette spiralled towards the ceiling. He did not know how long his mind had been away, and beset by the terrible fear that it might soon depart again, he backed down the passage and found the handle of the bathroom door.

Once inside the bathroom, his hands began a palsied trembling as he fumbled with the door-latch. It was a simple sliding latch, but it seemed to have a will of its own, and refused to slide into the slot. His hands grew slippery with sweat and he abandoned the operation. In a frenzy of mental and physical anguish, he let go completely. The demons stirred into rapid wakefulness and went howling through his mind. Scurrying to the rustic cabinet he ripped it open and reached in . . .

The bottle of meths was not there!

After some ten seconds of insane gaping disbelief, during which he experienced a lifetime of whimpering horror, he began a frantic search behind the taller articles in the cabinet, but there was no beautiful plastic bottle of meths. In a dark treacly fog, on the edge of total amnesia, he began a search of the bathroom. He reached in under the old tub and into the watery depths of the cistern; he plunged his hands, claw-like, into the laundry-basket, scattering soiled clothing across the floor, but the plastic bottle was not to be found. Finally too weak and spent to stand, he slid down the wall and buried his face in his hands.

10

i

It seemed that some giant unutterably alien rodent had built a nest here to spawn its young: this place he was in. The floor was littered with filthy scraps of rag, straw and noisome faecal droppings. Rubbish and filth had built up in the corners and around the skirting-board, so that the floor-space was only two-thirds of what it must once have been. There was no furniture in this place he was in, and it was dimly lighted by a smoking old-fashioned oil-lamp without a chimney which stood on a box beneath a grime-encrusted window with a broken upper pane, through which a single star shone like a hot bright eye. He sat in the filth with his back against a roughcast wall, trying to bridge the black gap of amnesia, listening to the pounding of his heart and the restless stirrings of the creatures rolled in dun-coloured blankets and sacking, looking for all the world like giant cocoons. He seemed to be awake in the midst of a nightmare!

The spluttering lamp threw strange dark shadows across the crumbling walls and ceiling, from which long cobwebs hung like dusty, blackened stalactites. As he watched, riddled with an unnameable fear, a lopsided door at the farther side of the den opened slowly, sending a tortured creaking across the intervening space. A dark form slipped through the darker gap, and crouched there, watching.

He found that to close his eyes was useless, for in the increasing anguish of conscious withdrawal, all was as clear as if viewed with physical sight. The thing that had entered through the door began to move slowly towards him, and the scream which rose in his throat emerged as a pitiful gurgle as he threw an arm across his eyes to shut out the horror of the thing which now stood over him. But the picture — the evil leer on the brown face beneath the shaven skull with its criss-cross pattern of scar-tissue — glimpsed for but a second, was stamped on his mind as though by a photographic process.

Then the thing spoke. 'The coast is clear, ou Whitey. The boere have gone the other way.'

Dropping his arm, he raised his eyes to the spectre that looked like Boon; then he reached out slowly and touched a leg, all the while gazing up into the face in a mute appeal for mercy.

'What's up, ou Whitey — you feel sick?'

The leg was solid and he knew that it really was Boon standing over him.

The skolly's face grew solemn with concern as he squatted down and peered closely. 'You don't look so good, ou pellie,' said Boon.

Feeling terribly lost and stupid, he found it difficult to smile at the curious and compassionate skolly. Strange thought-forms were moving through his mind: overlapping, interlocking spectres. The interchanging of this awful reality of *is* with the fantasy of *was*, rendered him on the verge of screaming insanity. There was a girl called Flower-Smoky-Rainbow drifting about on the rim of his mind; and another called Gertie-Manya was holding a bright purple bottle out of reach of a man called Whitey-Shadow-Dreamy. The man was screaming, and his voice was loud in this unreal place: *'Where am I, Boon? For fuck's sake tell me what is happening!'*

The evil face was very close. 'You don't remember, Whitey? You don't remember you was asleep in the bathroom?'

'Bathroom? *Bathroom?*'

'I can see you don't remember nothing. It's the vlam. I can smell you've been drinking the blue-ocean, ou pellie. It makes your brain *lam*. You was asleep in the bathroom—*sat!* The cops came and knocked on the front door of the house. Loud — bang — bang — *bang!* Maybe four o'clock this morning, when I was still sleeping in my room in the yard. You came running out and told me it was the boere. We ran through the back lanes, and came to this place that I know. But you don't remember nothing; I can see you don't remember. It's the vlam; it makes your brain *lam*.' Boon smiled his evil smile. 'The boere were looking for me; all day they have been looking for me. Fork hulle!'

Trembling and rattling, his teeth chattering out of control in his head, he looked at Boon, and then around the gloomy den, which, because it was real, became more terrifying. But Boon was there for company. He *must* keep talking, chatting. 'What time is it now, Boon? Whose place is this?'

'It's maybe five o'clock. This is nobody's place, ou Whitey.'

'Who are these people?'

'Outies, goffels, rookers. Old ones who have no place. The bulldozer broke their place, and now they sleep here. They have no people. This one here's a goffel.' Boon jerked the blanket from the inert form close to hand, to reveal a dishevelled, tattered female. The woman was awake, and she spat at him like an enraged cat, clawing at her blanket. 'Make a quick fuck for the Whitey,' Boon said, fiercely jovial, grabbing for her crotch. Spitting out a string of sizzling curses, she kicked at Boon's hand and got her blanket back. Pulling it over her head again, she subsided amid muffled mutterings.

'You cold, Whitey?' Boon asked, looking at him closely, the woman and the incident apparently forgotten.

He was icy, but it was not yet a physical thing: it sprang from the etheric core of his bones. 'I must have a drink, Boon. For Christ's sake, I must have a dop!' He tried to rise, but it was a hopeless, useless effort. Sitting with his head against the wall, watching the ghostly movements of the cobwebs, he felt totally beaten and strangely numb: nothing mattered any more. His eyes wandered around the den, and shafts of light beyond the normally visible spectrum darted at him from the vicinity of the flickering lamp, and the moving shadows had depth and thickness, like the flats of a stage setting.

'You got kroon for a dop, ou Whitey?'

Kroon — money. A chemical cell was activated, and he felt in the pocket of his shirt, but there was nothing there. The idea of the five rands he thought he had, was just another fantasy. He shook his head wearily.

'I'll see Mommy,' Boon said at length. 'Maybe she'll give a borrel for you . . . why you look at me so funny, Whitey?'

Pressing back against the wall, he watched the great purple horns curling out of Boon's head as the skolly backed fearfully towards the door, an expression of dismay and realisation on his face.

'You got vlam horries, Whitey,' Boon said thickly. 'You wait here, I'll get a borrel dop.'

With the terrifying realisation that Boon was about to leave him, he managed to get to his feet and follow him to the rickety door. Outside, it was damp and raw, and the mountain was hidden in a heavy misty blanket. He found himself in a rubble-strewn street — or rather what was once a street, but was now just an area strewn with broken bricks and concrete. Fifty feet away, with its blade solemnly lowered, stood a great dusty-green bull-dozer. Boon was moving away from him, and unable to follow on his bare feet, he watched the skolly merge with the misty darkness, to disappear like a swiftly-moving wraith. He called out in grief and anguish, but Boon was gone. Very soon, the raw dampness of the morning drove him back into the evil-smelling den, where he sat with his head hanging down between his knees.

Presently, there were sinister movements in the vicinity of his buttocks: either fleas or bugs — probably both — or whatever alien vermin would inhabit such a place. Then the movements — either actual or imagined — were in his beard, at his crotch. Getting painfully to his feet, he had a bout of maniacal scratching, which only served to divert the creatures all over his body. Finally, fatigued, he slumped down again and allowed the things to have a field-day, while the increasing coldness crept through the walls and entered his very marrow, so that the total iciness became psychosomatic. The only sounds were the stirrings of the null-people.

'Hello Whitey darling.'

Ah, the voices! He had been expecting *them.* And it was not the kewpie or Doctor Milly Mayhew who had spoken: this was a new voice. With his face pressed firmly against his knees, he waited for the picture of the new thing to appear in his mind. But in his mind there was only the picture of

Boon hurrying back with a bottle. Looking up at the cobwebby ceiling, he saw that there were no faces up there, no images of himself in a thousand past lives. Then a movement drew his attention, and he realised, with considerable relief, that it was the old goffel who had spoken. The broken-down old prostitute had uncovered her head, and was raised on her elbow.

'Djy soek 'n dop ou Whitey?' she whispered.

The toothless grinning gap in the flat, bruised black face sickened him for a moment, then he saw that there was genuine concern in the strange amber eyes. Nodding in encouragement, and with a broad wink, the woman scratched around beneath her blanket and came up with a bottle. Accepting it eagerly and tilting it quickly, he poured a good slug into his stomach. It was well-watered-down vlam, and it bounced back and went spraying from his mouth. Clamping his teeth against the return of the second swig, he managed to keep it down. The stuff grumbled and groaned in his stomach, but made not the slightest difference to his crumbling state of health. Taking a third swig, he handed the bottle back. The goffel accepted it without a further word, took a nip herself, then pulled the blanket back over her head. After a minute or so, he heard her snoring.

Thereafter, he sat in a state of increasing nausea. The vlam, and whatever else had been in the filthy oily bottle, had not been a good idea. The stench in the terrible den had become almost overpowering. And where was Boon? Boon . . . Boon . . . Boon! Where was the bastard? The skolly had probably got a bottle from Mommy Stilhuis, then run off to his vicious pals. Angry with the idea, he found that he was on his feet again, moving towards the door, through the belching and fart-stinks and the stench arising from the messes on the floor.

Jerking the door open, he crept out into a nether world of heavy dark-grey fog: the mountain mist had thickened and dropped to ground level. And more mist was rolling in from the Atlantic, so that there was nothing, nothing whatsoever to be seen. Even the bulldozer and the houses beyond — fifty yards away — had vanished. Faintly, as if coming from across light-years of deep space, was the intermittent mournful booing of the Mouille Point foghorn. Moving a few paces away from the building, he peered around, but there was no movement anywhere; no sign of a hurrying figure carrying a bottle. Never in all his life had he been so conscious of so protracted a loneliness. It was at that moment that he knew, with the absolute conviction that springs from a source of infinite depth and mystery within the human psyche, that before the sun rose on the new day, he would be dead, or so close to it as to be of no account. His mind went flickering back over his past life, and when the chill forewarning of death had passed, he began to chuckle, for life seemed such a short and pointless thing. Then he felt nothing at all: what was there to feel? Birth had been a painless entry into life and light; death, therefore, would be an envelopment by painless darkness — absolute and eternal. Perhaps the process had already started: this thick cloying fog, like a blanket — like a black shroud folding around him. For a moment he stood quite still, considering the idea. Then he stiffened, and his calm consideration of death was ousted by an upsurge of the powerful primitive desire to live. And this desire brought fear, for there was something out there in the fog: he could feel it; he could feel it looking at him! Something, which his mind told him was unutterably horrible and alien. His mind, filled with childhood, biblical pictures of dark, delivering angels who came for the damned, to drag the twisting screaming souls into the sulphury depths of hell!

Fearfully he peered about, trying to penetrate the thick, slow-moving blanket of fog. Then in a fold of the swirls, he caught a glimpse of something scaly and green. He felt relief washing over him like a perfumed zephyr: the bulldozer; the wet, green metal of the bulldozer! He gave a little giggle of pure relief; then turned to stone, unable even to scream as it came at him out of the fog. From some unknown source, a ray of light came to strike its malevolent ruby eyes. The snapping, hairy mandible was half a yard across, and the bloated grey-green body sagged low between the eight tall, bowed and jointed legs, glistening with long wet hairs. The giant spider looked at him for a moment, as if sizing him up, then it rushed forward; a filthy, massive thing, reeking with evil and hate. The onrush drove him back against the wall, then he was thrown to the ground, conscious only of something slimy and stinking which entered his mind, then slowly dissolved. He lay on the broken rubble, panting and weeping, awaiting the next attack. The heavy fog swirled and briefly lifted, and there was nothing there but the patient, silent bulldozer, the ruddy reflecting glass of its taillights twinkling. Slumping back against the wall, he cried out in anguish to God for the return of Boon.

Vaguely, he heard the sounds which herald the coming of day: the unenthusiastic barking of awakening dogs and the crowing of cocks, the occasional whine of a vehicle on the Eastern Boulevard, and in the deeper distance, the cheeky zip, zip, zip of tugboat whistles. Recovered somewhat, he began to crawl towards the door of the awful hovel, and only when he was at the door, and unable to escape in any direction, did he see them coming up behind him, only twenty yards away.

The four dark stumbling figures seemed to rise out of the very earth, the fog clinging to their bodies, then shredding as they waved their arms about and stumbled on towards their obvious destination,

Moving quickly now, he took the only avenue of escape open to him. He went indoors and crouched down in the darkest corner of the den. In a flash of sharp clarity, he knew who was arriving: it could only be them, in this place at this hour: *Oulemmus Regionis Sextae* and the Gympie Street Crew, who else, for now that his time was so near, in their manner the Lords of Fate were setting the stage for the Grand Finale for the retribution for his misspent life. He found that he was chuckling in a mad and knowing sort of way, nodding and muttering to himself: *Whom the gods wish to destroy they first make mad. Ek sal djou kry, witvark! The prophecy is about to be fulfilled!*

Drunken laughter and snatches of song from without broke his train of demented mutterings. The door was flung open, and the four men staggered in, accompanied by long tendrils of fog. Ou Lem had lost his great cap and his scarred skull gleamed in the lamp-light as he ranted and raved, kicking at the stirring forms of the old null-people. Once again, viciously, the blanket was ripped from the old goffel. She screamed and spat, then fear possessed her, and she cowered back against a filthy wall, while ou Lem stood over her, then snatched her bottle.

The other skollies, ugly brutes mad with dagga and vlam were ripping the blankets from the terrified and protesting old people. One of the gang, a tall powerful brute, found another, younger woman. Kneeling astride her body, the skolly ripped at her poor rags of clothing, then produced his brown, enormously erect penis and fell across the woman's naked hips.

Bedlam ensued as more people awakened, some dashing for the door, while others were held and searched for bottles. Crouched in his dark corner, the horries gone, driven off by the terror of reality, he watched the rape and the ravage, while a small urgent voice tried to communicate, to penetrate to the tiny cell of reason yet functioning in the depths of his brain: '*Move. Rush the door.*'

Rush the door? Ha! What hope had he in the face of four mad animals? He waited, hoping that the first blow from a heavy buckle would do the job, would deprive him of consciousness, shut out the awful scene and whatever was to follow.

The fornicator was well on the job, and the woman had quietened and ceased to struggle. For some reason, ou Lem had decided that he did not fancy his woman. Draining the bottle, the skolly cast it aside, then kicked the old goffel in the face. Bright blood squirted from her smashed nose. Screaming in agony, she curled herself into a ball, drawing the blanket over her head for its meagre protection.

The three rampaging, belt-swinging fiends moved deeper into the gloomy den, their loud animal cries adding to the already desperate scene. One of them began to urinate on the old goffel's blanket-covered head. It was a frothy horse-like piss, and the old woman yelled and turned on her stomach beneath her blanket.

A moment later, he knew that his turn had come, for the urinator had seen him! The man tapped ou Lem on the soulder and pointed. They both came closer, to peer in silence at his cowering form, as if hardly able to believe their drugged and crazy eyes.

Quite without reason or thought, but luckily in the right direction, he lunged up and forward. It was a final desperate act, motivated by deep-seated self-preservation and nothing else, for he was incapable of constructive thought. Conscious of the blur of faces, the whistling of belt-buckles and the cries of glee, he found himself outside in the fog, with the skollies behind him. Stumbling and scrambling, he moved across the rubble, quite unaware of the broken glass and sharp bricks cutting into his hands and feet. He could see nothing, and he did not know where he was heading. Falling between two mounds of rubble, and unable to rise, he lay there, awaiting for the descending buckles. *As quiet as death,* said the tiny voice of the kewpie. *They won't see you in the fog. Just another mound of rubble.*

For perhaps two minutes he lay pressed to the broken ground, almost choking in the effort to contain his breathing. He could hear the skollies calling to one another, close at hand, then further away. Closer. One of them almost stood on his hand, and he shrivelled, awaiting the descending buckle. But the man stepped away, and the calling voices grew distant. Getting to his knees, he wiped the blood from his face. He was frozen through, so there was little pain. Locating an unbroken bottle, he gripped it firmly by the neck and moved away from the poor humble den of the old null-people, searching the fog ahead for some sort of landmark.

A row of houses loomed up, dark and dismal-looking dwellings, offering no sign of an early kitchen light. Sucking in great gulps of raw damp air, he found himself in a lane, and crouching down, he rested. But reaction quickly set in, and he brought forth the contents of his stomach. The spew ran down his fine new shirt, but he was past caring now about anything so mundane. A dog barked suddenly and loudly in the yard behind him, and he stumbled on down the lane, not knowing where he was going, nor caring very much, for the dark thing was settling down upon him.

Some time later, through a chink in the dark curtain of his mind, he heard the distinctive whistling of skollies and the wild barking of big dogs. The dirt floor of the lane he was in gave way to the paved surface of a fairly wide street, sloping upwards in the direction of his travel. It rose sharply, and as he rounded a bend he heard the dogs coming up behind him. Running wildly now, gibbering and panting, he mumbled curses and half-forgotten prayers. A ragged opening appeared in a wall ahead of him: perhaps the entrance to a backyard; perhaps *sanctuary?* Forcing more speed into his failing legs, he went through the opening at a fast run — and smashed into a jagged-edged sheet of scarlet agony.

ii

It seemed to be a tiny old-world square, surrounded on three sides by gaunt Edwardian houses, shrouded in mist and early Sunday silence. Nothing moved in the square except the mist, which swirled silently about and above him, lifting and dropping, thickening to murky-grey, now a translucent pearly-grey, all the while clutching with clammy tendrils at his frozen body which lay on the icy cobbles. The square seemed to be the preserve of a solitary cat: a familiar-looking cat; a scruffy sway-backed skolly cat with a chewed ear and a single, baleful eye. The animal crouched in puffed-up warmth no more than a metre away from his face, watching him warily.

Whatever lay behind him, he was unable to see, nor could he turn round, for the slightest movement sent agony screaming through his parts. The blood trickling from a gash in his brow ran into his eyes, and the raw morning was seen as though through a rosy glass. Only by blinking occasionally was he able to keep his eyes clear. Generally speaking, the day was brighter, but since regaining consciousness, he had not seen or heard a single human being. Presumably the skollies had given up their drunken chase: he could hear neither their whistling nor the barking of their dogs; which was not all that comforting, for the brutes might very well be watching from some vantage point.

By way of diversion, he watched a tiny rivulet of blood creeping through a canyon of the cobbles, wending its way towards the crouching cat. The little red trickle reached the animal's paws, and the cat stepped back a pace, then came forward and sniffed at the blood, lapped at it—gingerly at first—then with considerable appetite. Not without fascination he watched the approaching cat, wondering what it would do when it reached his face.

There was blood in his eyes again, and he shut them for a moment. But the action only served to divert his attention to the bubbling pain in his chest. He could feel the blood and the fluids moving around in there, in places where they ought not to be, and every fifteen seconds or so the blood welled-up in his throat, and he had to open his mouth to allow it to escape, but gently, for he must lie very still.

He forced his eyes open, for he could smell the cat: that filthy, fishy alley-cat smell. He could feel the animal licking at his beard, and then it came into full view, and he was obliged to look into its single mattery eye. It was cruel and unfeeling, like all cats' eyes. Collecting a good mouthful of blood, he gobbed it into the cat's astonished face. The creature sprang away, gave him a Cyclopean glare, spat back at him and made off across the square.

Even while grinning at his success, he floated into a painless void and the dark thing with its swirling colours came down upon his mind.

But it seemed only an instant before the pain returned. He blinked his eyes to free them of the pink veil. The day was brighter, and Boon was standing there looking down at him. The skolly had a half-jack of vodka in his hand, and his battered face was a picture of bewilderment and concern. Boon cracked the seal of the bottle and knelt down beside him, and it was at that moment that the blood chose to well up in his throat and trickle from his mouth. He heard Boon's intake of breath as the skolly sat back on his heels. 'Christ, you hurt, Whitey. What happened, ou pellie?'

He managed to say that he had fallen, and that was all, for Boon's figure was beginning to waver and blur.

'You want a dop, Whitey?' Boon bent over him and allowed a little of the liquor to trickle into his open mouth. It burned like acid and he coughed and spluttered as a great pain washed over him. When the light returned, Boon was standing again, his face blank with confusion and indecision. Then he crouched down and put the bottle on the cobbles. 'I must cut a line, ou Whitey. Soon it will be daytime and there will be people here, and boere. I'll check you, ou pellie.' The skolly backed away, then turning abruptly he ran off into the thinning mist.

He made several journeys to the void of painless peace, and each time that he returned faces came to look down at him; silent brown faces, ever-interchanging. Then there was only one face—a tough-looking though calm, freckled face beneath a peaked cap. The policeman spoke to him, but he did not understand what was said. He was dreaming of an organ-grinder who was churning out demonic music, when other uniformed people came to disturb him. He felt himself rising, being lifted higher and higher in a nimbus of electric-blue agony. A scream crossed his pain-brittle mind, then blessedly he heard the rustle, and his angel came again to cover and protect him with her soft downy wings.

iii

Each time he tried to reach out to touch her, the white figure of the angel wavered and melted away. She had been doing this for some time: she would come to stand at his side, then either melt away again or change into a girl wearing a bright floral slax-suit or a jade-green cheongsam. He found it most disconcerting. It was however the way with angels he had to concede. Then the very time that he decided to ignore her, the angel didn't go away, but she did change — into a nurse. She bent over and looked into his eyes and smiled.

'Welcome back,' she said softly. 'Now you are to lie very still and quiet, You have an internal injury.' She moved about, adjusting the tubes and machines that surrounded his bed.

Only minutes later, a doctor arrived. He was a darkly intense young man with a great curly beard. He came around the screen with a sister, and with a brief nod, began an examination.

'Do you feel intense pain anywhere in your chest?' he growled.

Concentrating on his chest, he thought about it, but he felt no pain that could be called 'intense'. He shook his head.

After a further few minutes of examination and a check of the instruments, and having repeated the nurse's warning, the bearded giant went away with the sister, and he was left alone to consider the state of his health. It was a curious business, for he kept fading back and forth from a noon-day light to deep twilight. There was a thing that went up his nose and, he suspected, down into his innards. His left arm, in a plaster cast, lay inert at his side. He tried moving his fingers — they didn't work. But his right arm and hand, though bruised and sore, seemed otherwise in fairly good order. He was beginning to feel the creeping tendrils of pain, when the sister returned, carrying a stainless-steel kidney dish. Briskly efficient, she swabbed his arm and gave him a shot, and soon after, he began to drift away from reality.

iv

Perhaps a day or two after his arrival in the great hospital — he was not sure — emerging from an uninteresting, murky world, he found a tall, elderly porter standing at the bedside.

'Is jy Paul?' the man asked, pronouncing the name 'Pole'.

In his befuddled state it was some time before he got the gist of the question. 'My name is Paul Scott,' he said, at length.

The old porter switched to English. 'I have a parcel here,' he said, holding up a brownpaper bag. 'It was left at Reception by a Coloured girl, who asked for a Paul who had been picked up in District Six. I think that you are the only Paul who was picked up in that place.'

'What is in the packet?'

The old man peered into the bag. 'It is fruit, cigarettes and a letter.' It was addressed simply to Paul (Whitey).

'I believe that it is for me. Would you open it and give me the letter?' There was a funny, glad little fluttering in his stomach.

'I will do that, Paul Whitey. You have good friends.' The porter beamed as he passed the letter across. 'She is a very pretty girl.'

Weak and spent though he was, he checked the tears prickling behind his eyes when he saw the signature, written in a round, school-girlish hand, and the simple words above it:

Dear Paul,

I knew that you were badly hurt and in hospital. Boon was watching when they put you in the ambulance. They caught Boon, and they have taken ou Lem away also. I am very shy of going to the hospital, but perhaps I will visit you. If not, I will send you some things from time to time. My ou says that when you come out of hospital you can share his room until you are strong enough to travel to East London. You are always welcome here. Get well soon,

Your friend,
Gertie Smit.

Closing his eyes for a moment, he was conscious of the warm soft body of a girl called Manya, and the tantalizing fragrance of jasmine. Even though his mind was dull, the last moments he had spent with her in his arms were very real, then the porter was asking if he should pack the gifts in the top drawer of the locker, where he could reach them.

'That would be very good of you,' he said absently.

V

During the first week, the taciturn doctor came quite frequently, feeling here and there, grunting comments to the sister, then going away again as if he had been examining a cadaver rather than a living human being. And feeling more dead than alive, he was left mostly to himself in the warm euphoric embrace of sedation, his mind wandering down strange twilight byways spanning the past and the enigmatic, uncertain future. Then as his body mended itself, and the drugs were gradually withdrawn, he sank deeper into a state of apathy.

They took the machines and the screen away, and from his corner bed he had a good view of the large ward with its sick and suffering men. In the bed next to his own lay a middle-aged man with a pale, drawn face and a few wispy grey hairs on his head, who, he learned later, had had an operation to his anus and fortunately, preoccupied with the condition of his nether orifice, was disinclined to exercise his mouth. When the screen was removed, Piles looked him over briefly, closed his eyes again and lay as though dead. Though he commiserated inwardly with the suffering man, he was thankful that he was not expected to indulge in any small-talk. It was a few days before Piles offered him a brief 'Good-morning'.

On the day that he was allowed out of bed for the first time, the June rains started, and he sat at the window in abject misery, looking out at the rain-grey, dismal city below. Completely 'dried-out', he was conscious of returning physical health brought about by rest, medication and regular meals, but mentally he was depressed and withdrawn — and feeling weirdly unreal.

When he was able, he began making short sorties of the ward and environs, but he was disinclined to speak to anyone. He had an idea that he was looking for something, but only his subconscious mind knew what it was. When he had been up and about for about a week, sitting in his chair one morning, he was visited by the bearded doctor and a female social-worker, who introduced herself as Mrs Metz. She was a thick-set woman who stood on heavy, bowed legs, and her stern double-chinned face made it quite clear from the outset that there was to be no nonsense with her. For half an hour both she and the doctor gave him a torrid time about the evils of alcohol, and the agonizing end he could expect if he continued drinking. He had heard it all before, and the verbal bombardment only served to give him a splitting headache and set his nerves jangling to a pitch where he almost screamed at them to fuck-off and leave him to his misery. But he contained himself, and the session ended amicably enough.

His search had become a conscious operation, and that same afternoon he found what he had been looking for—in fact, he found two of them, and that night he had his recurring dream about being in the centre of an ever-expanding sphere of multi-coloured light. The two icy fingers came gently to close his eyelids, but not before he was presented with an incredible vision. When he awoke he gave a great laugh, which startled Piles and caused the suffering man to ring for the nurse.

'What are you laughing about so early in the morning?' the tired young night-sister asked, looking at him closely.

'I'm laughing because I'm the happiest man in the world. Last night I had a dream in which I saw quite clearly the utter insignificance of a single human life against the vast backdrop of eternal time and space.' He grinned broadly at Piles, who groaned and closed his eyes.

The night-sister looked at him blankly for a moment, then making a note on his chart, she warned him to be quiet, then went away, giving him a queer look over her shoulder.

The tension in him was broken. The depression lifted, and outdoors the winter sky cleared and the city was flooded by bright sunlight. Once more resolute, his mind at ease about the direction he would take when he was discharged, he loafed happily; reading and paging lazily through magazines. He even became quite friendly with the recovering Piles.

He had another session with the doctor—whose name he learned was Beamish—and Mrs Metz. It ended on a dramatic note when he told them that those of his relations who had not died of alcoholic poisoning, had either hanged themselves, or had been shot by the police. He had made this admission, having first asked forgiveness of his late father, Captain Paul Scott, Royal Navy, who might very well be gazing down from the bridge of some celestial battleship. The faces of the two do-gooders were a picture of conflicting disbelief and diffidence. And when they went away, he was a little sorry for the whopper he had told. But he grinned at Piles — the man had been eavesdropping — who called him over and gave him a toffee and confided in a whisper that his 'very own' mother had committed suicide because of alcoholic addiction.

vi

On a bright Friday afternoon — the eve of his discharge — he borrowed writing materials from Piles and wrote a letter to the Station Master at East London, requesting him to send his case carriage-forward to Cape Town Station. He signed his name with a flourish, for he was beginning to glow merrily, indeed. Enclosing the mangled baggage ticket, he sealed the envelope and went down to the Welfare Office.

Mrs Metz — who presumably had had reports of his increasingly sunny disposition — beamed upon him and studied him proudly, as an alchemist might who had created a rare substance from dross.

'I am glad to see you looking so well and happy, Paul. Since you're being discharged tomorrow, I was about to send for you. Doctor Beamish and I are very proud of the way that you have pulled yourself together. Yours has been a very unhappy background, but you're an intelligent and educated man and there is no reason why you should not put the past behind you and take your rightful place in society. All that is required is *will-power . . .'*

Despite the glow that was upon him, he winced at the expression she had used. Then he smiled his ugly smile, for physically Mrs Metz presented a double image. He blinked his eyes a couple of times, and she became one. But after a few moments, while she was scratching through the papers on her desk, her counter-part moved slightly to the left, and she continued speaking with two mouths.

'In special circumstances — very special circumstances, you understand — the Department issues rail-warrants to displaced persons who have been ill in hospital. I will be able to do something for you, Paul. so that you can go back to East London.' Mrs Metz's two faces were aglow with the pride of her good-works.

'I have decided not to go back to East London for a while, Mrs Metz.'

The good lady's two sets of heavy eyebrows shot up. 'Really! Why not, Paul?'

'I am going to stay with some friends in Cape Town.'

'Where in Cape Town?'

'Clifton,' he said without a qualm, for the glow was increasing.

'Clifton! Splendid! You'll be able to take long walks on the beach, Paul. Get as much sun as you can. And food. You must eat a lot of nourishing food. Keep yourself fit and strong . . .'

He said that he would do all of these things, then timing it perfectly— when Mrs Metz was beaming in her most expansive way — he bit her successfully for five rand, a pair of shoes and a jersey. He gave her his letter to post, then went up to the ward and re-read Manya's letter for the umpteenth time. Briefly closing his eyes, he recaptured the picture she made in her padded pink house-gown. Perhaps she would be at work when he arrived at La Residence Stilhuis in the morning. But no matter, Achmet Smit—perhaps even Mommy—would surely provide a can of soetes for the occasion. Shortly before supper, his drinking glass in the pocket of his gown, he strolled into the ablution section of the ward. Sliding open the door of a large cupboard, he reached in behind the large canisters of cleaning powders and liquids and found the plastic bottle. Then, quite certain that he had caught the sound of the whirring of tiny wings, he slipped into the bathroom and poured himself another big hooker of vlam.